Allow me to be Frank!

Prologue.

For as long as I can remember I've got into trouble and embarrassing situations even as a kid but as an adult
It's like someone up above is looking down and having a good old laugh at me.
This is why I've been given the nickname Frank Spencer.
All my calamities and scrapes I find myself in doesn't surprise my friends anymore they simply say 'it could only happen to you' or 'you should write a book'.
Il give you an example of a situation I found myself in just the other week.
While working away from home in Portsmouth.
I was living in a shared house with a workmate and a noisy fat bloke downstairs.
Anyway this particular day was scorching hot and I'd just finished washing my work gear we didn't have a dryer in our digs so I went outside into the glorious sunshine with my basket of wet clothes.
Unfortunately the fat bloke had beaten me to the washing line, his sheets and enormous boxer shorts were hanging on the line.
I decided to check if they were dry which they were so I decided to pluck them from the line.
I began to tug at the biggest purple pair of boxer shorts I'd ever seen and said out loud 'look at the size of them' while pulling them off the line.

To my horror when the pants were out of view I stood looking into next doors garden where a blonde lady in her 50s was sat sunbathing with enormous breasts only covered with a skimpy bikini top.

She looked at me open mouthed covered her breasts with her hands and ran quickly for cover in the kitchen shouting 'Geoff Geoff Geoff!' I ran like Usain Bolt out the house jumped in the car and sped off knowing my luck Geoff will be Hampshire's hardest man and be built like a brick shithouse!.

Chapter one.

Hammer Horror.

Friday
September 1997

I was starting my apprenticeship on Monday in a Shipyard called Wear Dock in Sunderland so I quit my job at McDonald's before they had the chance to sack me for my calamities.

It was Friday and I was sat at home with my Mam watching This morning in our house in our rough council estate in Sunderland.
The estate was well known for its villains and drug dealers.
Our little square was the exception a quiet little cul de sac was a friendly well-kept nice looking square, well that was until the family from hell moved in next door! They were well known drug dealers.
They were a young couple in their early twenties friendly enough always said hello when we passed them in the square but it was obvious to everyone they were dealing drugs as cars came and went all day and night.
Anyway this particular day me and my Mam were sitting having a coffee watching Telly when a rough looking lad in his early 20s appeared on a BMX he was very dodgy looking with a tatty old tracksuit and a hooded top pulled over his head.
As he cycled closer my Mam said
'Here comes the drugs!'
'You what?' I replied quite shocked.
'Every day same time someone turns up with a package for the druggies next door gives them a package then leaves' my Mam said pointing to the scruffy lad outside.
Today unexpectedly he stopped outside our house pulled his hood down
while climbing off his BMX as me and my Mam looked on in horror.
He unzipped his hooded top and pulled a claw hammer out and walked towards our door and rang the bell.
My Mam screamed 'go! Get out the back door!' Before I knew it my Mam had bolted the front door and practically dragged me to the back door.

My 14 year old sister came rushing down from upstairs to see what all the commotion was about.
My Mam wasted no time grabbed my sister by the arm dragged her into the back garden and shoved her into the old shed. She then pushed me to the back wall and shouted 'jump up! go find a phone and ring the police! quick ' she screamed while shoving me towards the back wall.
Somehow I managed to scramble up the six foot wall but to add to my worries once I was on the top I realized the other side was a good 12 foot drop into thorny rose bushes. Without a lot of time to think and adrenaline pumping I jumped into the rosebushes which sent pains all over my body as the thorns tore into my flesh and worse still I was now dangling like a puppet by my

ripped Sunderland home shirt.

I eventually managed to wriggle myself free and drop landed into a pile of mud beneath my feet
I ran like Lynford Christie to the new estate behind our house where my best mate Pikey lived
within a minutes I was at his house, I jumped over the gate and burst into his front door where
Pikey was sitting in his boxer shorts watching Richard and Judy.

He looked at me and started laughing his head off and said 'fuck sake   Andy what you done
now!'

I tried to explain as quickly as I could but he just sat there laughing at me with a Sunderland
shirt ripped to shreds and covered in blood and muck.

As I didn't get the help I was looking for I ran into his kitchen and seen his golf club set and I
picked up the biggest looking club I could find and bolted out the door.

Aware Pikey didn't have a phone I ran next door to his neighbor's house where nosey Rosey
lived, I banged on her front door and shouted help as Pikey looked on out of the window
laughing his head off.

Rosey came to the door eventually and looked at me with shock

'Are you okay son? What's happened?' She said pulling a twig out of my hair.

I explained as quickly as I could and told her to ring the police which she did immediately.

In my state of panic I suddenly realized my sister and mother are at the mercy of this maniac so
I shot off out the door with the golf club to my family's aid.

I somehow gathered my thoughts as I got to the edge of our square and became aware of the
danger I was in and decided to peek round the corner towards our house.

He was still there at our door with hammer in hand with his back to me, I sprinted as fast as I
could towards him and made a quick grab for his hood and swung him round onto the grass
where he fell into a heap and dropped the hammer.

I raised the club above my head ready to take a swing at him.

He looked up at me with a look of fear etched across his spotty face.

'What the hell are you doing?' I screamed into his increasingly familiar face.

In that moment three police cars came screeching into the square followed by a van with its
sirens blaring.

My Mam opened the front door and shouted 'that's him that's the druggie!'

Pointing to the panic stricken lad on the grass.

Then he looked at me and said 'I've only come to bring your dad his hammer back'.

My Mam suddenly looked over all confused at the lad on the grass and said

'John? Is that you?'

I looked at my Mam lost for words my Mam read my confused look and shouted 'John! It's Lisa's
John!'

My heart sank as I looked at all the police cars in the square and the realization filtering through
that my cousins new boyfriend john had come to return my dad's hammer he must have
borrowed.

Chapter 2
Day one at the shipyard.

The induction.

The sun was shining as I was standing in the number eleven bus shelter over the road from my house.
I would almost be able to enjoy the weather if it wasn't for the smell of stale piss in the old stone bus shelter.
I was suddenly awoke from my thoughts as
the double decker bus hissed to a stop and nearly made me shit my pants in fright.
It was my first day at the dockyard as an apprentice plumber.
I felt I'd finally succeeded in life no more working in MacDonald's or burger vans as much as I loved the food and the female attention it was now time for a proper job as my dad would say.

Yes today this 20 year old lanky skinny boy was going to be a marine plumber/pipefitter after my apprenticeship that is.

As I boarded the bus I noticed Ricky a lad of 16 who lived round the corner from me, he was at the job interview the day I had mine a few month back.

 'Areet mate' he said
'You got the job then?'

'aye pipe-fitter what about you?'

 'Welder' he replied.

Ricky had just left school this year and this was to be his first job, I knew this as he was in the same school as my sister Natalie who fancied him.
It was the staring roll as Danny in Pennywell schools production of Greese that clinched her undying love as she put it.
How could he play Danny? I thought with blonde curtains haircut!.

'I thought your dad worked at the dock, what ya doing getting the bus?' Ricky asked

'He's useless he was on the drink last night can't get him up and I don't want to be late my first day'
I replied.
We chatted for a while mainly about football and how useless Sunderland were at the weekend.

We finally got off the bus at the city Centre as far as the bus went.

A quick stop off for fags and papers and we headed down Hendon bank a manky run down area of Sunderland that lead us to the docks.

Suddenly a clapped out maroon ford fiesta pulled up next to us and beeped its horn, 'Jump in lads' a voice shouted out the window.

'Aright blue, how's it going?' Ricky said to the old grey haired scruffy looking driver.
As I climbed over the back seat I recognized the driver as one of my mates from school Wayne's dad.

'Cheers' I said as I struggled to climb in over the bent over front seat into the back.

'Fawlty's son ain't ya?"
Blue asked as Ricky pushed the front seat back too quick nearly breaking my legs in the process.

'Aaaaaaaaiii!' I struggled to reply as the pain shot down my leg.

'Fawlty?' Ricky muttered as blue interrupted

'Thought it was you, I heard ya were starting, ya used to hang around with our Wayne years ago didn't ya?'
Blue asked

'That's right' I said remembering what a nutter his son was at school.

'He's a bailiff now, still daft as a brush though,
he was up at the flats up gilly law repossessing someone's telly the other week, and was banging like fuck on someone's door on the top floor, they wouldn't answer so he just gave up, when he got to the bottom the bloke threw his telly over the balcony and shouted 'there's the fucking telly' just missed him smashing to pieces and then our Wayne shouts up 'you got the remote mate?'
To which we all started laughing!!
As the car stopped at the security gate house.

'Areet adolf' blue said to one of the security blokes.
'whose these two?' The security asked pointing to me and Ricky,

'Couple of new saveloys starting today' blue replied, me and Ricky looked at each other puzzle as he opened up the gate crossing the road.
'Thick as the yellow pages him' blue said as he drove through the gate.

'Never guess what happened the other week' he said
'one of the lads Billy, mad he is always nicking stuff, anyway he was walking up the bank every night with a wheel barrow with a old rag covering the top, every night the security lifted the rag

and shone the torch in seen it was empty and let him through, this happened every night for a fortnight, he was too thick to realize he was only nicking wheelbarrows!'.

'Here we are boys! Welcome to wear dock!'
Blue said.
'Cheers' me and Ricky both said as blue headed off towards a manky looking canteen.

'Hey why do they call him blue?' I asked Ricky.
'Blue Peter! he's a right dirty old bastard, sound though couldn't meet a nicer bloke, he's a good mate of my dads'.

An hour later we found ourselves in the health and safety induction room a small, stuffy room with no windows
or ventilation! only a door at either end and an overhead projector lighting the room and six sweaty board looking new apprentices sat round a big white table.

A tall skinny Clark Kent geeky looking bloke came in wearing white overalls with a shirt and tie underneath.
'Good morning lads! my names Gavin i am your shafety officer, I'm here today to teach you all about shafety in the workplace' he said with a lisp which made a few of the lads chuckle.

'Lets leave all the jokes outside I'm here today on serious business to teach you about shafety!' Gavin said looking annoyed Which added to the giggles especially every time he used the word "shafety".

We all sat nodding off listening Gavin's boring voice babbling on about the various hazards of working in a shipyard! he made it sound like we were stepping into the world of bomb disposal.

His gory slideshow of various injuries that can happen was the only thing that kept us from nodding off, with the exception of Ricky who I kept nudging with my elbow in his ribs each time he fell asleep.

After an hour of gory slide shows and health questionnaires Gavin shouted 'ok lads were gonna take a short break, help yourself to tea and coffee next door, and those of you who want to kill yourselves feel free to smoke in the workshop' he said pointing to the other door.

Three of us headed for a fag out of one door and Ricky and the other two headed out the opposite door for drinks.

'Wanna tube?' one of the lads said in a thick Geordie accent passing a cigarette to myself and a small strange looking kid with dark hair and beady eyes.

'Cheers! Andy by the way mate" I said as I pulled a lighter out my pocket and passed it round.

'I'm Iain' he replied lighting his fag up.
 'You both Mackems?' Iain asked

'Why aye!' I replied

The other lad muttered something about needing a dump and wandered off.

'What planet he's from I've no idea?'
 I said. Pointing to the strange kid as he wandered out the workshop.

'You a Geordie?' I asked Iain

'I'm a sand dancer me man, I'm from south Sheilds'
 He said.

Just then my dad wandered through the big gates leading to the workshop. I quickly dropped my fag and covered it with me foot.

'Shit my dad!'
I whispered

 'Does he not know ya smoke like?'
Iain asked laughing

'Na and he'd fucking kill me if he found out' I said with a worried look on my face.

'Aright son' my dad said

'Aright' I replied

'Ian, dad, dad Iain' I said

'bit of a tosser that Gavin bloke isn't he' Ian said then takes another drag on his fag.

'Gavin na he's alright him man, bit of a jobs worth like but he's ok, wait till ya meet photo finish now he's a tosser' my dad said.

'Photo finish?' me and Ian said at the same time looking puzzled.

'You'll understand when ya see him, John West is his name or tuna some of the lads call him, right prick though watch him he's been known to sack lads for fuck all.' My dad muttered

I looked a bit shocked not used to hearing my dad swear, Ian laughed looking at me.

'Those things will kill you son' my dad said watching Ian put his fag out.

'disgusting habit' I said smirking

Just as Iain looked as if he was about to spill the beans Gavin's voice shouted 'right ladies back to business get your arses back in'

My dad winked and walked out of workshop with a pipe over his shoulder, me and Ian wander into induction room.

'Where's Colin?' Gavin asked me and Iain we both shrug our shoulders 'dunno who's Colin?' Iain mutters

'Right anyway lads we've got the head of shafety in this yard coming in to give you's a talk so I want you to show him a bit more respect than you've shown me' Gavin snapped

Just then the door opened and a bloke in his late 50s walked through the door with an unbelievable hunch in his back his head looking down to the ground.

Suddenly Ian started laughing his head off, I looked over he points at the bloke who walked in and mutters 'photo finish' which sets me off and I suddenly burst out laughing!! The laughter becomes infectious and before long the whole room is in stitches.
Just then a nervous looking women in her late forties walks in smartly dressed with a tray of sandwiches she carefully places in the middle of the table looking puzzled to why everyone is in hysterics.

'What on earth is so funny?' photo finish asks looking straight into my eyes.

'Erm, erm father ted!' I replied with the first thing that entered my head
'we were just talking about Father ted that was on last night'

'I seen it' Ricky laughed 'Chris the sheep' to which one of the other lads made sheep noises "Baaaa"
"Baaaaaa" one of the other lads joined in with an amazingly accurate impersonation of a sheep which set the room into hysterics again.

'I shagged a sheep once, was gonna stop but it kept asking for maaaaaa!' Iain shouted now with tears of laughter rolling down his cheeks.
the rest of the lads were starting to see how pissed off photo finish and Gavin were and they were trying to stop themselves laughing but to no avail, when suddenly photo finish slams his fist on the table sending the plate of sandwiches all over the table. The room was suddenly silenced except for Iain burst out laughing pointing to the sandwiches scattered all over the table

he shouts 'there fucking tuna!'
The room was in uproar now
Everyone in kinks of laughter,
suddenly the door to the workshop opened and in walked the strange beady eyed kid looking puzzled why everyone was laughing.
Gavin shouts over to him 'where the hell have you been Colin?'
'For a shite I got locked in' his reply.

Gavin looked at photo finish and said 'where in god's name did they drag this lot from?'

"Cherry knowle?" photo finish mutters Under his breath and stormed out.

When things eventually settled down Gavin told us how lucky we were to be given the opportunity to earn a trade and how photo finish (John west) was so close to sacking the lot of us over the outbursts.

The mood in the stuffy room was now as cold as the coffee
'Right now I want you all to go and collect your P.P.E from the store' shouted Gavin

'Ppe?'Replied Colin with a confused look on his face.

"Personal protective equipment!" replied Gavin 'which you would have known if you had the intelligence to open a toilet door'
Gavin snapped

'Head through the workshop door turn left into the big shed and you will see a big sign if you can read! It says "general stores!".

As we all Stepped into workshop a group of scruffy looking blokes including my Dad were gathered round the work bench giving us the once over.

A small fat dark haired bloke in his forties shouted 'which one is your boy fawlty?, Wait See if I can guess!' he said pointing to Colin 'him'

'No, he looks more like your kid him' my dad said laughing

He did too both had dark hair beady eyes and quite chubby in fact Colin had everything but the drinkers red face.

'Him' he said pointing to me.
'That's my boy!' my dad said pointing to me.

'Looks nothing like you, must be the milkman's' he laughed.

Then he came over 'na just kidding son, I'm john cotton or dot as the lads call me' he said with an outstretched hand
'Andy' I replied shaking his, while thinking has everyone got a nickname here?

'how's it going?' He asked

'Aright,' I replied 'just off to get out ppe from the stores'

'You couldn't do me a favor could ya?' He asked, 'will you pick something up for me while your there?'

Before I could answer he blurted out 'cheers just ask for a long stand, ask Larry he will know what I'm on about, cheers young en just leave it on the bench for me!' He said pointing to a work bench in the corner.

By now all the apprentices had wandered out the workshop, I quickly ran after them and spotted them gathered inside one of the main manky looking old building. I wandered through the big double doors and joined the back of the Queue to the store.

A friendly old face popped through the hatch asking for each apprentices name and each time then handed them a big cardboard box containing two pairs of overalls a helmet, safety glasses and a bag of other bits and bobs, I wondered how the hell I was going to manage to carry all that as well as the long stand thing for Dot.

My turn eventually came, and the friendly looking old bloke that had Ron written in black marker pen on his hat said 'hello bonny lad what's your name?' smiling as he asked.
 'Andy Carter' I replied
 'Ah you must be fawlty's son! he said you were starting, good lad your old man' he said smiling.

Then I remembered about dot, 'is Larry about?' I asked.
 'I'm your man' he said 'what can I do you for?' He said laughing!!

Puzzled why he had Ron on his hat I asked 'how come you have Ron on your hat if your called Larry?'

'That's my helmets name' he laughed
'Only joking, the cheeky buggers here call me Larry because I'm always happy, you know the term happy as Larry? he laughed well that's me Larry' he said trailing off chuckling away to himself.

'Anyway' I said 'dot asked me to ask you if I can have a long stand for him'

'No problem' he said 'just give me a few ticks while I quickly serve these lads here and il sort you out bonny lad' he said then proceeded to serve one of the scruffy looking blokes in the que.

After about ten minutes all the lads had wandered back to the induction room I was starting to get a bit worried.

'What's happening Larry?' I asked

'don't worry bonny lad I haven't forgot about you, il be with you shortly' Larry laughed.

About another ten or fifteen minutes later a scruffy black and white looking cat wandered up to me brushing its head up my leg and moving between my legs making a loud pitched meow!.

Larry popped his head out the hatch 'ah here he comes for his dinner' and disappeared again for a few minutes then came out with two bowls one with cat food in and the other with milk with the word 'Bastard' wrote on each bowl in marker pen.

'Here son put these on the floor for bastard will ya?' Larry said handing me the two bowls as I placed them on the floor the cat shot from my leg and started happily munching on his dinner.

I went back to the hatch and noticed Larry had gone
'Larry, Larry!' I shouted through the hatch 'coming' he shouted.

Then five minutes later Larry appeared with my boxes of ppe and dropped them into my open arms.

'Give me two minutes' he said 'and il get your long stand'

Shit I thought it's been ages all ready.
 Just then there was a Big Bang when the double doors at the front of the building opened, Bastard the cat ran off with fright.
 I looked up and noticed Gavin walking towards me with a well pissed off looking face on him!.

'What the hell's taking you so long? you've been gone half an hour' Gavin snarled.

'I've been getting something for Dot'
 I replied sheepishly not wanting to add fuel to his already burning rage.

'Let me guess tartan paint, solar power torch?' he shouted.

'No' I replied 'long stand'

'Long stand!' Gavin hissed 'oldest one in the book!' hey your as thick as your fatha you boy!!!".
'Has your stand been long enough?' Gavin asked charging off ahead not waiting for my answer

Back in the induction room it was form filling in time.

'Right lads I want you all to fill one of these forms in' Gavin said passing the forms round to each of the apprentices 'hand them back in then you can go for your dinner, one of you can pop out of the yard to get sandwiches for the rest of the lads'.

We all finished filling forms in except Colin who seemed to be struggling. Gavin wandered over to see what was taking so long.

'What's happening Colin?' Gavin asked

'Erm er I haven't got my glasses' he replied 'I can't make out what it says'

'Here' Gavin says and hands him a magnifying glass from his top draw.

Colin pulled a panicking face so Me and Iain went over putting two and two together that he couldn't read or write. Luckily Gavin left the room and We helped him fill out the form. I had to alter it a couple of times as Iain kept writing things he shouldn't like where it said Address he wrote 'no thanks I wear trousers'.

The other lads were too busy to notice, they were deciding what they were having for dinner and writing it on a sheet of A4 paper Gavin gave them.

After a few minutes or so Dan one of the apprentices came over asking us what we wanted for dinner and gave us the pen and the paper to write on our orders. Ian shouted 'just get me a crocodile sandwich and make it snappy'.

I grabbed the paper wrote on Andy 'cheese chip buttie' then Iain grabbed the paper and scribbled something on
Then asked Colin what he wanted.

'll just have a sausage roll please' Colin replied.
Iain folded the paper over and wrote something on the front.

And said 'right Colin you get yourself up the shop out the way' and gave him the note.
 'Just give the note to the woman in the shop mate' Iain said.
Colin picked up the pile of money off the table and reluctantly agreed and wandered out the room.

Just then Gavin returned 'where's he gone?' I replied 'he's gone to the shop, ya said he could! there's his forms he's done them.' I said giving Gavin Colin's forms
'look at the state of that! There's more scribble on there than writing' Gavin moaned.

'Why the hell did you send that numpty to the shop? He'll probably get lost' Gavin snapped shaking his head while walking out the room.

Thirty minutes later we were all sitting in our bait hut hungry wondering where the hell Colin was!.

'Where the fucks he gone to get the bait Newcastle ?' Ricky shouted

'I'm starving wish he'd fucking hurry up!' One of the other lads snapped.

Just then the bait room door opened 'right lads back to induction' Gavin shouted 'Haway man'
'fuck off!'
'never had nee bait yet!'
came the shouts from the apprentices.

'What you on about where's Colin?'
Gavin shouted.

'Hasn't came back yet!' shouted one of the quieter apprentices.

'Told ya he'd get lost' Gavin laughed for the first time today.
'Anyway come on lads soon as we get this paperwork done the sooner you can go!'.

Suddenly the bait room emptied everyone getting the impression we could go home when were done.

'She seems in a happier mood' said Iain

The good mood didn't last though when we got outside a police car turned up with Colin in the back.

'Good god what's he done now'
said Gavin.

Back in the induction room ten minutes or so later,
'Of all the stupid pranks!! I can't believe one of you could do this' photo finish ranted

'Immature and downright disgraceful' added Gavin

'and you Colin you should have told us you can't read or write'
said Gavin.

Colin sat there like he had the world on his shoulders.

'Give me all your money I have a gun in my pocket! You're lucky there not pressing charges!' photo finish said with a face of bewilderment

'Tomorrow I want whoever responsible to go up to the shop and apologize to the poor girl. Otherwise this will not be the end of this, I may even think of getting the lot of you replaced.' Photo finish yelled then walked out and slammed the door behind him.

'Right lads' Gavin snapped 'get out of my sight! Tomorrow is a new day Anymore stupidity and you're out' Gavin shouted pointing to the door.

As we were walking out the door my dad stopped me.
'What's this about an armed robbery on the greasy spoon cafe?' he said laughing

'one of the lads sent Colin (who can't read) with a note saying I have a gun in my pocket give me all your money'
I replied.

'Wasn't anything to do with you was it?' He said laughing

'No'
'Good your mam will go mental if you get sacked!' He said
'tell her I'm going to be late home I'm working till six' he said walking away laughing.

I noticed Iain and Ricky walking up ahead laughing and carrying on so I jogged to catch them up,

'Go on bet ya can't do it again' Ricky
Was shouting at Iain

'Fiver says I can' Iain replied

'Go on then' taunted Ricky.

'Right' Iain said opening out his arms out preparing himself, then suddenly spat out his chewing gum caught it sweetly on his right foot and kicked it up in the air and caught it in his mouth. Me and Ricky started laughing as we headed up the bank towards the security gate.

Just then Ricky started giggling
'What's up?'
Ian asked
'Look!'
Ricky said
Pointing to the bloke with the wheel barrow with the old rag over it which I set me off laughing.

Iain looked puzzled as me and Ricky walked through the security gate in kinks of laughter.

Chapter 3
Day 2 at the shipyard.

Tools of the trade.

Johnny Cash was blasting out of my dads clapped out Volvo, with my dad singing top of his voice with me in the passenger seat as we headed through the security gates to the dockyard 'Morning Adolf' my dad shouted out the window to the security guard as he waved us through.

As we pulled into the car park a bright yellow souped up Citroen saxo skidded to a stop next to us with hardcore dance music blasting out the windows.

'Morning Fawlty' said the tall stocky in his early 20s leaping out the saxo

'Morning Decka' my dad shouted back sticking his head out the window

'Watch out for him Andrew, he's a nutcase' my dad told me as the lad walked on ahead.

'How's that like?' I asked as we climbed out the car

'He smacked his boss at Amec' he said 'knocked him clean out'

'Why?' I asked

'His mam rang him in sick because his dog died, and his boss said tell the soft git to get himself in, he got himself in alright and chinned his boss! he even drew round him in chalk as he lay on the shop floor!' My dad laughed
'it was there for months after, he got the sack like, half way through his apprenticeship, but these felt sorry for him and gave him a chance to finish his apprenticeship here, canny kid just a bit radio rental' he said

'Radio rental?' I asked

'bloody mental!' my dad replied heading off towards his canteen.

I walked into the apprentices bait room but didn't notice Iain sneaking up behind me shouting 'morning lads' in a camp squeaky voice then jumped out of sight so it looked to everyone inside that I'd said it.
Everyone stopped talking and looked at me like a weirdo then carried on talking.

Iain walked in a couple minutes later with a serious face 'morning lads'
'Twat' I said laughing

'Hey you'll not believe what I've just seen' Iain shouted

'What?' Colin asked

'Seen bastard the cat having a shit and you never guess what it did after? It only started burying its shit!'
Iain said looking astonished

'All cats do that man!' Colin shouted back

'what with a shovel?' Iain said laughing
Everyone started laughing except Colin who just looked out of the window puzzled.

'You going for the bait today Colin?'
Dan asked Colin laughing

'I don't think so' Colin replied looking annoyed.

'Hey where's Ricky?' Iain asked me

'He's not coming in he's got chicken pox' I replied

'Chicken pox? How old is he ten?' Iain laughed

"Pringles" Colin shouted

'Eh?, what's he on about' Dan shouted

'Adults don't get chicken pox! They get Pringles!' Colin stated

"Pringles?" Iain laughed
"Shingles" you daft twat Dan shouted with everyone laughing

'hope he doesn't pop his spots if he's got Pringles hey Colin?' Iain laughed 'because once you pop you can't stop' Iain said laughing which sent the rest of the lads in fits of laughter as the bait room door opened and Gavin stood in the doorway looking bemused,

'Alright lads! just a quick word' Gavin shouted.

'Right! Quiet down, today's the day you start work, pipefitters stay here and wait for John, welders come with me il take you to the welders bays to meet Ronnie, all other trades follow me Gavin shouted turning to walk out leaving only me and Iain left in the cabin.
I lit a cigarette and passed it to Iain then lit one for myself. I took one drag then the door opened and my dad walked in I quickly dropped the fag onto the floor and covered it with my foot.

'you'll get shot smoking in here young en if they catch ya' my dad said to Iain
'Anyway Andrew, ya mam said she put my bait in your rucksack' he said grabbing my rucksack off the table and started  rummaging through it.

'yours is the Morrison's carrier bag' I said

'How come you get a yoghurt like?' He muttered while raking through my bag "salt and vinegar!" My dad shouts 'how come I get bloody ready salted' he said looking annoyed while still raking round 'and a bloody Twix' he shouts shaking his head 'going to have words with her! shocking' he shouts while storming out the bait room with his Morrison's carrier slamming the door.

Iain starts laughing 'must be mad working with your dad' Iain said

'I know it's going to be mental' I replied.

Just then the door slams open and a tall stocky bloke with penny glasses and "J.J" wrote on his helmet storms in 'you the pipefitters?' He shouts

'Yes, you john?' I ask

"Names" he shouts with a touch of venom in his voice I immediately took a disliking to this bloke I thought.

"Andy Carter" I replied coldly

'Andy? What were you christened with Andy were you?' he muttered while writing in a notepad 'fawlty's son aren't you?' he asked.
'Yep' I replied

'most of the lads got in here because they stuck in at school but you got in through the backdoor ey Andrew?' He replied with a sinister look in his eyes.

'bloody hell who is this knob-head? I whispered to Iain as John wrote something in his notepad

'your name?' he said looking over the top of his glasses in Iain's direction

"Iain" he replied
'Fucks sake! Iain who?' John snapped back

"Hunt" Ian replied looking at me with a look of what the hell is this guys problem?.

'you can wipe those dumb looks off your faces laurel and hardy your not at school now' he shouted and walked out slamming the door.

Iain and me looked at each other 'does the prick want us to follow him?' I asked

Iain shrugged his shoulders 'he never said, fuck him' Iain said passing me a fag.

Just as we sat back down enjoying our smokes the door burst open and john looking furious ran over and grabbed me and Iain by our ears dragging us outside screaming.

John dragged us to a manky looking dark and dingy workshop with all shapes and sizes of pipe on the bench and a stench of oil and dust.

'This is your home for three years kids, while your here you do as I say understood?'
John shouted

We shrugged our shoulders
'Understood?' John snapped grabbing our elbows and squeezing our funny bones which sent a shooting pain up our arms

'Aghhhhh!what ya deeing man?" Iain shouted

Just then Decka walked in the workshop seeing him latched on to mine and Ian's arms 'hey John you bullying kids again?'.
'Decka there worse than you these useless twats look at them it's Dumb and Dumber!' John snapped back shaking his head looking at us.

'right Andrew you get me a shifter!! and Iain you get me a hacksaw and see me on the office roof in five minutes' John shouted and stormed out of the plumbers workshop.

'What a bell end!' Decka laughed looking at me and Iain stood there looking gob smacked.

'Don't let the prick get to you he was like that with the second year apprentices the lads told me, try that with me il knock his teeth out!' Decka said

'He can't get away with that can he?' I asked

'Bloody hell man you better deal with it' Decka snapped
'he threw a lettuce at me yesterday and that was just the tip of the iceberg' Decka laughed and walked out.

I laughed at the size of this guy rather than his joke, he was only in his early 20s but was built like a brick shithouse his shoulders where huge.

'What the fucks a shifter?' Iain looked at me puzzled

'Where we gonna get this stuff?' I asked Iain back.

We walked out of the plumbers shop not knowing what to do next.

'What a prick how can he get away with talking to us like that'
I said

'Fuck him just take the money' Iain said looking unaffected by the whole scenario and wandered off muttering
'I'm going for a shite'.

I headed into the big fitters shed which I knew the store was in there somewhere!.
As I walked through the door I forgot there was a bottom part to it and tripped over sending my helmet rolling and me crashing to the ground nose first.
roars of laughter erupted from inside as I lifted my head off the oily floor.

'Young fawlty' dot shouted
'Just like ya fatha' he said as the rest laughed.

I slipped and slided trying to get up of the oily floor each time falling back down, now my overalls where covered in oil.

'Where will I get a hacksaw from?' I asked struggling to my feet.

'B&Q one of the lads gathered round dot shouted as the other blokes all laughed

'Haway I shouted I went to the store to get your long stand the least you can do is lend me a Hacksaw' I snapped back amazed at my attitude thinking the fall must have unlocked some long awaited confidence as I finally managed to get to my feet dripping with oil.
Dot laughed reaching over into a big blue box and as he opened it a yoghurt shot out and covered dot 'what the fuck!' dot shouted looking at his tool box with all the lads gathered round him laughing their heads off.
Seeing a now empty yoghurt pot taped to a hacksaw blade which was bent back under the weight of the lid and duck taped to the front end of the box, i got the impression Dot liked being the prankster not the victim, dot was looking a mixture of embarrassment and anger when he handed me the hacksaw. 'look after it and remember where it lives'
he said handing me the hacksaw with yogurt dripping from his chin.

'Cheers' I replied trying to contain my laughter of one of the best practical jokes id ever seen, feeling a little triumphant after the long stand incident, i hurried out the fitters shed knowing John didn't seem the patient type.

I wandered down towards the office and
to the right of me i noticed a scarily big old wooden ladder leading up to the roof, just then I seen John stick his horrible head over the side of the roof shouting

'where you been?'
'bloody hell man just like your fatha!'.

Shit! I thought wish I had a quid for every time I heard that since I started here.
'Get up here then! what you waiting for?' shouted John.
At this point I felt like saying enough is enough I'm going home but just remembered my days at McDonald's being shouted at by some jumped up prick.
At least this dickhead has been there and learned how to be a dick I thought no matter how hard its going to be these three years had to be done!, I'm sick of being treat like shit" I'm going to be someone even if it is just a plumber I thought.
My thoughts where Rudely awoken by John shouting down the ladder 'you on something?'
Here goes I thought as I climbed the ladder shitting myself thinking I can't give this prick the satisfaction of knowing I'm scared of heights. i climbed the ladder grabbing on as if my life depended on it while shaking like a shitting dog all the way up leaving a trail of oil behind me.
'scared of heights as well as thick as shit?' God help us' he shouted shaking his head looking down the ladder at me clinging on for my dear life.
I climbed up of the top of the ladder and headed over to the opposite side of the roof where John was bent over the opposite edge doing something with the drain pipe.
'Give me the hacksaw young en'
John shouted
'What's with all the oil?' he asked
'I tripped over in the shed, the bloody floors covered in oil!' I said hoping for a twinge of sympathy
'Bloody hopeless' John muttered to himself as
I walked over to him handing out the hacksaw.
'Where did you get this? Look at the state of it! covered in bloody oil!' he moaned as he bent over the edge of the roof with his arm moving backwards and forwards in a cutting motion
'And where's your mate?' He shouted
'Dunno!' I replied on the verge of turning round going back down the ladder and never seeing this shithole again!.

After twenty minutes or so of him handing me bits of plastic pipe bunged up with muddy green slurry and insults which made me feel like jumping off the roof
John shouted
'Where the fucks your mate?'
'I don't know!'
I shouted back defensively trying to escape further wrath from this prick
'Thirty minutes he's been gone to get a shifter' John shouted in my face spraying my face with spit.

What seemed like an hour later I peered over the edge and seen Iain walking in our direction as John paced behind me shouting abuse, and to my horror I looked to Iain's right hand and I seen what He was carrying "a hacksaw!"
'Oh shit' I thought as

I reached over the side trying to do my best mime act signaling to Ditch the hacksaw and go get a shifter, whatever the bloody hell it was!

But it was too late Iain just climbed the ladder looking up without a care in the world.

John noticed me looking over the side curious to what I was looking at he looked over the edge and he spotted it

"Hacksaw!" That's it!

Go! go! Get out my sight useless!'

John shouted pushing me towards the ladder.

Iain grabbed the ladder and began to climb up, I looked at John straight in the eye only for him to shout

Go on fuck off! Hopeless, hopeless!'

John shouted taking off his helmet and throwing it In my direction! missing me by inches,

I quickly descended the ladder just wanting to get as far away from this prick as soon as possible.

Iain screamed up to me 'ahhhhh! what ya deeing man?' as I stood on his hand,

'Sorry mate!' I shouted but it was too late Iain let out another shout and fell about three meters to the ground,

'You alright mate?' I shouted down looking at Iain lying on the muddy ground

'Aye hard as nails me man!' Iain shouted back dusting himself off shaking the hand I just stood on. I started laughing so bad that in turn made Iain start laughing the two of us were buckled laughing.

After finally calming down after a proper giggles fit I said

'bloody hell we drew the short straw with him haven't we?' I said as I jumped off the ladder

'unreal him like!' Iain said

'Fancy a Belly buster?' Iain asked

'Aye why not' I replied

As we walked Iain kicked a stone which whizzed off ahead 'hey did ya see that man?' these steel toe capped boots are quality for kicking stones fancy a bet?' Ian said

'Why Aye!' I agreed 'bet I can send one further' I said.

Iain took a run and kicked a stone and sent it shooting towards the crane.

'Beat that!' he said looking proud.

I braced myself and seen a steel nut on the ground, I thought that would do better than a stone and swung back my right foot with all the power I could muster and wham!!! I hit it only unexpectedly it was somehow fixed to the ground and when I kicked it the thing didn't move! I did however screamed like a baby and fell screaming grabbing my possible broken toe

'ahhhhhhhh!' I screamed

Iain was bent over with laughter.

I finally got myself to my feet with agony in my right foot, I looked behind me John was staring from the rooftop open mouthed shaking his head with his hands on his hips.

'Frank Spencer you man' Ian laughed as John looked on stunned.

We eventually arrived at the very scruffy looking burger van a women in her fifties overweight and incredibly small stuck her head out the hatch and said
'What can I get you boys?' in a broad Scottish accent.
Decka burst through the queue and shouted 'two chicken legs open!' Me and Ian laugh but the Scottish woman looked at Decka unamused and says
'New boys?' she said looking towards us with a Purvey grin. 'Aye new apprentices full of horny young hormones just for you Alyson!' Decka laughed
Me and Iain just grinned shyly.
A couple of minutes later the burger woman hands Decka the biggest sandwich I've ever seen in a half stottie bun with bacon, sausage, egg tomato, beans, black pudding you name it dribbling out the side
'One belly buster' Alison shouted and handed it to Decka.
He opened his mouth and took a bite sending egg yolk dripping down his chin
'lovely that sweetheart' Decka shouted with his mouth full and handed her two pound coins and walked off.
I stepped up and said 'one belly buster without tomato or black pudding with brown sauce' I said reluctantly seeing the size of the thing thinking it will take me a week to finish it.
She nodded and turned to make my sandwich.
Iain shoved his way forward and said 'il just have a chip buttie' and is your vinegar free?' he asked winking at me
'Of course it is' Alison replied
'Well I'll take four bottles then' Iain replied laughing.
Again I erupted into fits of laughter!
Iain laughed as Alison turned away to make his chip buttie, Iain ceasing his chance undone the vinegar bottle top leaving it loosely sitting on top of the bottle.
Colin behind us shouted over 'can i have cheesy chip buttie please?' 'You can wait your bloody turn first' Alyson snapped to Colin handing me my belly buster.
I had to use both hands it was so big,
I squashed it down with my hands so I could get my mouth round it sending egg and beans dribbling all over the counter
'look at the bloody mess you made on my counter!' Alyson screamed as she handed Ian his chip buttie.
I grabbed some serviettes and began wiping up my mess just as Alyson handed Colin his cheesy chip buttie,
Colin grabbed the vinegar pouring it all over the chips! The top fell on his chips and the vinegar went everywhere! all over the counter I'd just cleaned, Colin was covered in it!
'Bloody hell man' Colin shouted 'I'm gonna stink'
'That's it clear off! The lot of you' Alison shouted.
Iain and me set off in kinks of laughter again
'What about my chip buttie? my buns all soggy!' we heard Colin shouting at Alison as we walked away still giggling to ourselves.
'Who's serving at the burger van today?'

blue shouted to us from a distance.

'Alison, I think her name is' I shouted back

'Get in!' Blue shouted pulling a comb out his pocket running it through his scruffy grey hair and sprinted off towards the burger van.

Iain and me both laughed as we headed over to the bait room.

As we burst into the bait room I done loud cat squeal noise which made everyone jump.

Just as we sat down Colin walked in with a face like thunder.

'What's up with Colin?' Dan asked.

'He Got covered in vinegar at the burger van, Iain loosened the top and col used it' I laughed as Colin stripped off his overalls and wandered to the sink washing the vinegar off his hands and face.

Dan laughed with a mouthful of coke dribbling down his chin.

Just then John burst through the door reaching over grabbing Ian's ear then mine 'agghhh what now?'

Ian shouted

'Breaks over, out!'

John shouted dragging me and Iain to the door by our ears.

Finally letting go outside the plumbers shop he said 'right there's a ship come in get yourselves down to the dock, Il see you by the man rider in five minutes' he shouted storming off towards the fitters shed.

'Bloody hell I can't take much more of him' I said looking at Iain lighting a fag

'Want one mate?' He asked handing me a cigarette

' Cheers' I said taking one out of his outstretched packet.

As we walked smoking and chatting we passed the crane and seen the big grey navel ship sitting in the dock with a big sign painted on the side saying "orange leaf"

We walked out of the sunlight into the shade of the crane, when suddenly felt little spots of water on our faces.

'Is that rain?' I said looking at Ian confused as there didn't seem to be a cloud in the sky.

'Ughhhh! That tastes like piss!' Ian shouted spitting out what just went in his mouth. As we got to the edge of the crane we made the mistake of looking up seeing Billy Animal the crane driver pissing over the rail up at the top of the crane singing 'we're singing in the rain were singing in the rain' top of his voice.

'Haway man' Iain shouts up brushing the spray off his overalls with the back of his hand

'Dirty bastard!' I said shaking the piss off my helmet.

As we walked further forward alongside the ship I asked

'how we gonna get on board?' looking around noticing there was no gangway to the boat

'Didn't John say something about a man rider?' Iain asked.

Just then I spotted John storming towards us.

'Right get in' John ordered pointing to a big cage with a door either side with a wooden floor.

We walked through the door as John attached a hook to the top and waved up to billy to lower the crane down to pick the hook up.

'Bloody hell, we going in this?' I screeched.

'Stop being such a fanny' John snapped back while hooking the crane to the top of our man rider.

Suddenly it lifted sharply off the ground and swung left and right as it got higher and higher. I gripped as tight as possible onto the handrail as Iain looked on laughing at me looking petrified.

John pulled a little black walkie talkie out of his overall pocket 'Billy Animal call back' he shouted into it while holding onto the button

'Billy animal eh!' Came the muffled reply on the radio

'Stop mucking about Billy and drop us on the aft end!' John shouted down the radio as we seemed to be heading towards the end of the dock swinging and swaying as the crane moved down the tracks with Billy shouting something out of the window and laughing.

We looked down over the edge we were now being lowered down over the water at the end of the dock gate.

'What's he doing the bloody idiot' John shouted as he raised his radio to his mouth

'Billy Jonson call back' John shouted

'Can't quite hear ya John!' Came the reply as we got closer to the water

'Lift us on the aft end' John shouted down the radio.

John was getting redder and redder in the face by the minute.

The crane eased down really slowly towards the water I looked over the dockside and looked at a crowd of blokes including my Dad and Dot laughing their heads off as the cage dipped into the water, our boots underwater now it kept on going till the water got to our knees and then john's radio cackled and Billy's voice came over the radio..

'is that aft enough for you John?'

'Stop clowning about and get us on deck, you bloody idiot' John shouted down the radio.

After a couple of minutes the crane finally lifted us on the the back end of the boat with John shouting and swearing up to Billy in the crane.

'Bloody idiot!, speaking of which, Andrew, Iain there's a couple of shifters I want you to take that pipe out, we got to take it back to pipe shop to remake it!! Il be back in five minutes' he shouted pointing to a small copper looking pipe that ran along the side of the ship and he walked away leaving us looking puzzled!.

'And make sure you isolate it first' john shouted sticking his neck round the corner.

'What's he on about isolate it?' asked Iain

'No idea' I replied

After about five minutes of wondering what to do I opened the shifting spanner to the same size as the nut on the pipe and began to turn the nut, but it wouldn't budge. Iain had a go and it started to turn he kept turning slowly till the pipe started to feel loose and a few drips of water started to come out.

'Il see If I can find a bucket' Iain said giving me the spanners.

I carried on where he left off turning the nut slowly when all of a sudden the spanner flew out my hand and water started gushing out everywhere soaking me and everything in the area and it wasn't stopping,

"Iain!!!"

I screamed but no sign of him,

the water kept gushing out! I was now up to my ankles in water with the water showing no sign of stopping

'What the bloody hell you done now!' John shouted running round the corner.

He ran towards me and shoved me aside sending me flying into the water flat on my back.

'told you to isolate it you bloody idiot!' He shouted,

He quickly moved his hand about a meter from where the water was gushing out and turned a valve and the water stopped.

John turned to me with water dripping down his face 'get away from me now!!!'

I jumped to my soggy feet and just as I was about to get out of there Iain came round the corner with the smallest bucket I've ever seen

'Found one' he said.

John took one look at him and shot towards him. Iain dropped the bucket and ran away from him

'Get here!'

He shouted while chasing him down the corridor swinging his foot to try kick him up the arse! I decided to run off in the other direction, luckily I noticed there was now a gangway in place which I quickly ran across to the dockside.

As I looked across I seen John chasing Iain along the side of the boat, finally John gave up the chase and Ian seen the gangway and ran towards it.

As he seen me on the dockside he started laughing and that set me off the two of us headed towards the pipe shop laughing our heads off.

'I'm going for a shit' Iain said

Thinking probably best if we keep out of johns way for the rest of the day I thought I'd better go too.

'So am I' I said and followed Iain into a manky looking toilet block it had a vile stench with five or six cubicles and a urinal overflowing obviously blocked but nobody bothered to fix.

Ian went for the end cubicle, all the others were full apart from the one next door so I went to that one.

As I walked in I saw Ian's head as the cubicle walls were so low. He looked at me and laughed.

I sat on the manky bog not needing to go just hiding from John so just sat reading the graffiti on the wall. The bit that caught my eye was "toilet tennis look right" I looked right and on the other wall in the same hand writing said "look left" .

'Hughhhhhh!!'I heard coming from Iain's bog an extra loud strain noise he made then a plop then he shouted 'areeet'

'Areeet?' I shouted back

'Ya hughhhhhhhh! Going out tonight' he shouted while straining again with a plop sound at the end.

'After the nightmare today i need a drink. 'hughhhhhhh!'Iain shouted 'Me too' I shouted back

'You coming round mine then?' Ian shouted

'You what? you live miles away' I shouted back

Just then Iain popped his head over the side and said 'I'm on the phone to my lass here you know!. can ya keep it down a bit!'.

About an hour later I was on my way to my dads car to head home after a nightmare day, I was walking with my dad and Decka

'Don't know if I can handle working here much longer' I said

'Don't let that prick spoil it for you' Decka said

'I've heard he's going in for photo finishes job anyway as a shafety manager so he'll not be bothering you for much longer' my dad said imitating Gavin's lisp.

'thank god for that' I thought as we jumped in the car and Johnny Cash Ring of fire came on blasting.

Chapter 4
Day 3
Wet dream.

I was awaken from my deep sleep by heavy thumping on my bedroom door and my dad yelling 'Get up ya tit! We've slept in'
'Good start to my day!' I thought as I climbed out of bed and headed towards the bathroom.
'No time for a wash we're late man!' My dad shouted While struggling to pull his jumper on 'Ya work in a shipyard not the Ritz ya handbag!' He screamed as he ran downstairs.
I ran into my room and sprayed some Lynx on and quickly jumped into a pair of old jeans and an old naff naff jumper and pulled on my old trainers.
I ran down the stairs past my younger sister smirking on the settee and i ran in the kitchen my mam handed me two rucksacks and put a piece of toast in my mouth!
'Hurry up your dad will be going mad' she said quickly pushing me towards the door kissing me on the cheek.
 I charged out of the door ignoring my sister shaking her head at me.
After slamming the door shut I ran towards my dads clapped out Volvo he was beeping his horn shouting out of the window 'Haway man hurry up' i was just about to get in when my foot slipped on something soft and squishy and I fell to the ground, I quickly got myself up off the ground and quickly dusted myself down and jumped into the passenger seat of the car and before I even had a chance to get my seat belt on my dad skidded out of our cul de sac with Johnny cash boy named Sue playing full blast.

'Have you shit?' My dad shouted at me,
'No'
I snapped back, 'Well something stinks in here, You better have not trod dog shit in!' My dad looked at me with a suspicious look on his face.

A couple of minutes later my dad pulled in at a bus stop
'What we stopping here for like?' I asked
'We're picking dicky Don King up' my dad snapped back.

'Hey what you snapping at me for? It's not my fault were late' I shouted
'Your the one with the decent alarm clock, you know ours is cream crackered!,'
My dad snapped.
'If the druggies next doors dog shut up I might have got some sleep, the noise was worse than when you come in pissed!'
I snapped back,
'You can less ya lip an all or you can walk to work'
He snarled

The back door of the car opened and a grey haired bloke in his late fifties jumped in
'Aright basil, you must be young Fawlty?' he shouted reaching across to shake
My hand!. 'What's that smell?' Dicky asked

'You bloody have shit haven't you?' My dad screamed at me 'open that window it's stinks' he shouted at me pointing to my window.
'How was your weekend away like Dicky? Amsterdam ya went wasn't it? On the ferry?'
My dad asked peering in his rear view mirror.
'You don't wanna know Billy
Bloody nightmare from the start' Dicky replied.

'How's that like?' my dad asked then slammed the breaks on and shouted out the window 'watch where you're going you silly cow!
Bloody women drivers should be banned the lot of em' my dad muttered under his breath as he looked up to Dicky in the mirror,
'Aye the wife insisted on taking the bloody dog!, we only just set sail and the bloody thing jumped off the aft end into the water!'

'Bloody hell you're joking?' my dad replied half laughing.

'Honest! They wouldn't turn round the bastards, So I had to put up with her crying all weekend about the dog, ruined our weekend'
Dicky moaned
'But hey you'll never guess what was waiting for us on the doorstep when we got back home?'
Dicky asked

'The Dog' I shouted excitedly
'No' replied Dickie 'six pints of milk! the silly cow only forgot to cancel the milk as well'.

I climbed out of the car and headed for the bait room leaving my dad and Dickie at the car as knowing what John was like I was bound to be in trouble.

I got to the bait hut and opened the door there wasn't a soul in sight they all must be already out at work I thought,
I got to my locker which now had a cock drawn on it in marker I noticed, I opened the locker and took off my jacket and threw it in the locker and kicked off my trainers into the locker forgetting about my earlier incident I now noticed the brown sticky dog shit all over my trainers and now all over my jacket and locker i shouted 'bollocks!'
When I heard Iain's voice coming through the door.
He walked in to see what was happening and started laughing his head off when I showed him the mess.
'Never mind that Johns going mental that your late! You better get your finger out'
Iain warned.
I quickly put on my boots overalls and helmet and threw my rucksack in the locker without thinking straight on top of the shitty trainers.
'Ahhhh bollocks!' I shouted again and slammed the locker door.
Iain lit two fags passing me one while laughing.
Just as I took a drag the door burst open!. I panicked thinking it was my Dad and dropped it to

the floor covering it with my boot, Iain however wasn't so quick.

'smoking in here you animal, people eat in here ya dick!' John shouted.

He then grabbed the two of us and shoved us to the door and kicked me up the arse.

When we got outside John said to Iain 'right you piss off to see Tommy the brush tell him you're gonna clean the bogs' pointing him in the direction of the big shed doors,

'And you young Basil I have a job even you couldn't fuck up' he said while dragging me towards the ship.

When he eventually let go we walked side by side in an awkward silence.

John broke the silence with an insult surprisingly 'so how come you can't get to work on time like everyone else?'

'I was kept up all night with next doors dog barking' I replied.

He reached in his pocket and pulled out a small packet of ear plugs and handed them to me, 'Put them in tonight because if your late again your getting a warning!'. I really couldn't stand this bloke I thought as we headed for the gangway. Once on the ship he took me down a few sets of stairs into a small room with a metal hatch open on the deck.

'Right listen to me' John shouted while shining the torch into the tank. 'This is a freshwater tank we have to fill it manually' and pointed to a big blue hose pipe that was already hanging over the edge into the tank tied loosely to a metal handle to stop it moving.

'Nightshift have filled three quarters of it now your going to fill it to that mark there!' He Pointed to a line clearly marked in the tank. He gave me a little walkie talkie type radio. 'Here take this, now I'm going to turn the water on all you have to do is sit here don't move and soon as the water reaches that level you shout of me on the radio and I'll turn the water off, it's probably going to take a couple of hours so get comfortable' he said and began to walk away.

'Any problem radio for me, you think you can manage that?' John shouted sarcastically.

'Yes' I answered as he stormed out

'Dick' I said

He immediately came back in and slapped me across the back of my neck!.

And take your finger off the button as the whole yard just heard you calling me a dick!' He said pointing to the radio I had in my hand.

'Shit sorry'

I said

'You will be' he said with a deadly serious looking face and stormed out

'Dick' I said again this time making sure I didn't have my finger on the radio button.

After a few seconds water came gushing out the hose into the tank I was no mathematician but figured this was gonna take hours I pulled up a bag of rags and plonked it onto a wooden shelf about a meter above the deck and sat on it staring at the water coming out of the hose.

It was going to be a long day I thought and began chucking bolts into a bucket to amuse myself, once I got bored of that I sat back got myself comfortable on the bag of rags and began pondering life.

Suddenly I woke up with a jump, realizing I must have dozed off I looked down to my horror the tank wasn't only full it was over flowing and the room I was in was flooded!

'Shit shit shit! Think think!' I shouted out.

I tried to think what I could do but quickly gave up I picked up the radio and braced myself I was in trouble big trouble I thought.

All I could do was admit what I'd done I thought and apologize

'John call back' I shouted into the radio pressing the button 'I don't fucking believe this that baldy prick is going to kill me! I shouted' then to add to my woes I realized I never released the button!.

'John John the tanks full' I shouted panicking trying to redeem myself.

Then the call came back

'I heard everything what you said Andrew, I'm on my way over!'

'Shit my life is over' I thought.

I sat there terrified awaiting my wrath.


After a few minutes of waiting Decka walked in the door above the stairs and immediately started laughing

'What the fucks happened here?'


'I fell asleep johns gonna kill me and I called him a baldy prick over the radio'. Suddenly John came barging past Decka and charged down the stairs and plunged into the water and plodged his way towards me with his face red and a look of intense rage on his face, he tried to climb onto the shelf but slipped into the water and fell totally submerged in the water! he threw his helmet across the room and charged again at me this time getting onto the shelf grabbing my legs as I tried to wriggle away! he yanked me off the shelf into the water and pulled his fist to punch me.

Decka quickly hurtled down the stairs and dove on John and dragged him off me and jabbed him in the ribs, John was raging but he saw sense he knew he was out of his depth and couldn't fight Decka who stood over him fist raised

'Your gonna get sacked for this!' he screamed at Decka as he winced in pain, then looked at me 'and you!'.

I was in panic mode I apologized and pleaded with John not to sack Decka it was me at fault not him but Decka looked at me winked smiling and suddenly backhanded me across the face.

I looked at him shocked already feeling a bruise swelling under my right eye.

'That's gonna leave a mark that on young fawlty's face where you smacked him John' Decka said

'Who's gonna believe I did that?'.

John shouted back

'Well I saw you with my own eyes so did he didn't you Andy?' Decka looked at me urging the answer out of me.

'Yes' I said quickly fearing Deckas look in his eyes. 'I'm a fair man John,

You say nothing about this we will get this water pumped out and I'll not break every bone in your body if you keep Shtum' Decka snarled staring intensely into johns eyes. John weighed up his options gave me the filthiest look and said 'This place better be spotless before today's out or your a gonna!' and  he quickly stormed out leaving me and Decka knee deep in water.

Soon as John was out of sight Decka burst out laughing pulling out a box of soaking wet fags out of his pocket and he handed one to me all soggy and bent and said 'you got a light?' Which set me off laughing.

After ten minutes or so Decka left and came back shortly after with a big heavy hose on his broad shoulders and threw it to the deck into the water making an almighty splash 'That should do it' Decka said wiping a spot of mud off his shoulder, 'Jesus that looked like it weighed a ton!' I said looking on amazed. Already the water was disappearing into the hose. 'Decka I'm sorry for getting you in this mess with me, I appreciate the help though cheers mate' I said. 'It's no bother man! Besides I got to take that dickhead down a peg or two, if there's one thing I can't stand it's bullies and that pricks been getting away with it for years'.

My opinion changed of Decka as we sat watching the water suck up the hose. He seemed like a nice lad a sort of gentle giant but I seen today he's not to be messed with. 'Sorry about the eye by the way looks like your gonna get a black eye, I hit ya harder than I meant too' he said looking at the swelling around my right eye. 'No bother, hey you don't reckon John will say out do ya?' I asked. 'Na not if he knows what's good for him, but hey let's keep this to ourselves I know what he's like he won't want to lose face, if word gets out he might see his arse and grass us'. 'il not say a word mate, cheers I owe you one' I replied.

The water now was nearing the point to where it should have been originally and I was going round sucking excess water out of corners of the room with a wet vac just as John walked in and seen me busy and Decka manhandling the hose out of the tank.

'Is that level ok John or do you want more water out?' Decka asked John as if nothing had happened. 'aye that's fine cheers Decka' John replied nervously. 'look john, sorry about earlier it went a bit too far but hey look it's spotless in here no harm done eh? and we won't say nowt if you don't'. John thought for a second and said 'Aye I suppose so' And walked out. Decka looked at me and winked 'see told ya sweet as a nut'.

Half an hour later I headed into the bait hut and walked in the other apprentices looked at me and laughed at me dripping wet. 'you been swimming?' Dan asked 'You could say that' I laughed just as the door burst open and Iain came bursting in with a fish in his hands on a bit of fishing wire. 'Hey look what I've just caught' he announced proudly. 'Where did you catch that? The river?' Colin asked

'No it was running along the jetty' Iain replied sarcastically.

'Obviously the river you thick twat!'

Everyone burst out laughing.

Iain headed to the fridge and popped the fish in just as John and photo finish and the welding foreman walked in the door.

My heart sank I had the feeling John had blabbed about the flood incident.

'Right quiet lads and sit down' photo finish shouted in a very serious tone.

I sat there fearing the worst when to my surprise photo finish announced there was going to be an owners walk around so they wanted the place spotless, all the apprentices were to be given different areas to sweep up.

John slammed a list on the table 'right Dumb and Dumber you two sweep the outer decks' and he handed me and Iain a dustpan and brush each 'Colin you sweep the Bridge' and he gave him a dustpan and brush and stood staring at us 'what you waiting for? Go on piss off' he shouted as he shoved us out the door.


Me Iain and Colin did as we were told and headed down towards the boat kicking stones as we went.

We approached the gangway and me and Iain walked on board but Colin wandered off past the gangway Iain looked at me and gave me a puzzled look 'where's he going?'

I shrugged my shoulders and we started sweeping the deck.

Iain started doing pull ups on a pipe that ran across the the deck head.

After about five or six he said 'how many can you do?'.

I gave it a go struggling to get even one.

Iain started laughing 'you can't even do one?' and he jumped up and done another six or seven with ease.

'Watch out here's john' I shouted as I seen him walking down towards the gangway.

Iain quickly dropped down and dropped down to his knees with the dustpan gathering the muck while I swept it onto his pan.

Suddenly out of character John started laughing his head off, me and Iain looked at each other shocked until John pointed over to Colin in the distance sweeping the bridge over the river.


John took off his penny glasses and wiped a tear from his eye, seeing him without his glasses on for the first time gave me a surprise and seeing his little beady nasty little eyes made me chuckle.

He shot a look at me and said

'What?'

'Colin' I replied looking across at Iain he was pulling a funny face I suddenly burst out laughing he glared at me again 'you laughing at me?'

'No, No! Colin' I replied and suddenly got a fit of giggles which I couldn't stop I looked over at Iain who had turned away but I could see his shoulders moving up and down, 'shit he's got them too' I thought while John stared at me. 'You fucking are laughing at me'

'I'm not' I tried to get the words out but couldn't contain my laughter then I heard Iain give a big howl.

John grabbed his shoulder and spun him around to see him in hysterics red faced and tears rolling down his eyes

'What you laughing at?' He screamed at Iain 'have you opened your mouth?' John asked staring at me 'no honest!' I said trying to stop myself laughing but then seen Iain in the corner of my eye and couldn't stop myself I was in kinks and the harder I tried the worse it got 'you fucking have haven't you' John snapped and swung a kick at me I swerved out the way of it and ran to try get away from him as he chased me around the deck I ran as quickly as I could turning as many corners as I could til he was out of sight. John eventually gave up and
walked off the boat red faced. Iain looked on confused and creased with laughter.

About an hour later I headed up to the workshop I'd been hiding on the ship out of johns way for what felt like ages but I had to head up there to get ready to go.
As I crept into the bait hut I seen Iain in my locker.
'what you doing?' He started laughing and removed the fish he'd caught earlier
'I was going to hide this in your locker'
Then he pulled a face as if he'd just remembered something
'hey Ricky's off isn't he?' He grabbed a knife from the sink and began working it in Ricky's locker and after a little wiggle here and there he popped the lock 'champion!' he said as the door swung open he then popped the fish in Ricky's right rigger boot and placed his overalls neatly over the top. We laughed then got ready to leave.
As we were walking out the door I noticed my dads car just outside the plumbers shop to my right 'hurry up ya tit!' my dad shouted.
See you in the morning bud I laughed and jumped in my dads car.
'Another day over, thank god!' I thought, only another two years eleven month and twenty days to go till my apprenticeship was over. If only I knew then what I know now that time would go by so quickly and when it's over you'll wish it was back again.

Chapter 5
Family Matters.

'Its 3 o'clock in the Bastard morning man!'

I awoke hearing my dad screaming out his bedroom window.
I jumped out of bed and pulled back my curtains to see what was going on. Just outside of the square was about four or five kids in there late teens drinking bottles of cheap cider with rave music blaring out of a ghetto blaster in the old bus shelter.
One of my neighbor's lights came on
and Harry from two doors down appeared at his front door with only his boxer shorts and slippers on and a cricket bat over his shoulder. He charged out towards the bus stop with a look of pure rage on his face.
'Bit late to be playing cricket ain't it Harry?' My dad yelled out the window as Harry stormed out of the square and crossed the road to the bus stop. He walked up to the kids stereo and smashed it to bits with the cricket bat then began swinging it towards one of the kids heads missing only by an inch at the most. The kids dispersed and ran off in different directions as Harry kept on swinging away at them as they ran off in different directions.
He smashed one across the back of the head as he ran off Then he charged back towards the square. My dad applauded out the window and whistled as did somebody else a couple of doors up the other way.
Harry didn't even acknowledge them he just walked in the house and slammed the front door behind him nearly smashing the little windows on the top with the force.

I jumped back into bed and pulled the quilt over my head and tried to get back to sleep.
Just as I was dozing off the Bastard dog next door started barking.

After tossing and turning for hours I finally decided to give up and get out of bed.
The carry on at the bus stop then the dog barking then the bloody house phone rang all meant I had absolutely no sleep I was knackered.
I jumped out of bed chucked a t shirt on and headed down stairs, to my surprise my dad was sat on the settee drinking a cup of coffee fully dressed.
'What you doing up its only 5 o'clock?' I asked my dad while rubbing the sleep out my eyes.
'Your gonna have to get the bus in today I've got to go in early, nightshift rang
One of my pipes leaked there'll be hell on if it's not fixed before dayshift come in, there meant to be going on sea trials the weekend!' he yawned
'Il just come in early I can't sleep anyway with that bloody dog next door, I'll just drink coffee and read my book in the bait room' I replied.
'You better hurry up then because I'm leaving in a minute'.
I quickly darted upstairs and got ready and ran out the door and jumped in the car.

The journey to work was quiet with my dad yawning and radio 2 playing and a posh woman's voice talking about how it was going to be heavy rain up and down the country. It seemed strange pulling into the security gate in the dark but the security guard just waved us through. We pulled up in the car park to the Dockyard and my Dad jumped out and wandered towards his locker room.

I wandered in the opposite direction towards our bait hut and opened the door.

I nearly jumped out my skin when I opened the door and noticed somebody was lying on one of the long wooden seats with jackets lay over the top of him.

'Shit sorry' I shouted with a jump. Assuming one of the night shift lads was having a kip. To my surprise

Colin popped his head out from beneath the jackets and said 'shit have i slept in?'

'What you doing here col?' I asked as Colin sat up and the jackets fell to the floor.

Colin sat up put his elbows on the table and put his head in his hands and started sobbing.

'What's up mate?' I asked while sitting down next to him and putting my hand on his shoulder.

'Nothing' Colin snapped and hid his face.

'I'm gonna make a coffee do you want one?' I asked.

'Aye please' Colin replied rubbing his face looking all embarrassed.

I boiled the kettle and poured a spoon full of cheap coffee into two manky cups I found next to the sink

'how many sugars Colin?

'Six' came his reply.

'Six' I laughed to myself.

I took the two cups over to the table and Colin shot a look at the cup with disgust.

'I'm not drinking out of that!'

'Sorry I should have cleaned it mate'.

'It's not that!' He said 'look it's got a Newcastle badge on' and pushed the cup away.

'So what's up mate? Haway you can tell me I won't say a word I promise' I said looking at Colin genuinely meaning every word.

Colin sat for a little while staring at the table flicking a crumb.

'Things aren't so good at home, my stepdad is a piss head keeps hitting my mam and picking on me, I've had enough of it that's why I've been sleeping here'

'Shit sorry mate,' I replied shocked.

'Have you not told your real dad?' I asked 'maybe he'll sort him out!'.

Colin just stared at the table and said 'I don't know my real dad he pissed off years before I was born'. I looked a bit confused then carried on

'Is your Mam ok? does he beat her bad like?'.

Colin looked at me and just put his head down.

We sat in silence for a little while I drank my coffee and he looked up and said 'please don't say anything'.

'I won't' I replied offering him a fag. Just then the door burst open and Dot appeared I quickly dropped my fag in my coffee. 'Where's my hacksaw fawlty?'.

Shit I'd forgotten all about that I thought.

'Johns got it, I think' I told him.

'I want it back! I needed it this morning you prick! We had to cut your dad's cowboy job out!'.

'Il have a look on the roof, John was cutting the guttering up there, he had it last'.

'Don't go blaming JJ, you fucking borrowed it'.Dot snapped back storming out slamming the door behind him.

'Fancy coming down the office with me like col? I'm gonna have to see if I can find his hacksaw'.

'Aye might as well' he said standing up grabbing his jacket off the floor.

We headed out the door and slowly walked down towards the office

'So how did you manage to get the job in here Colin?'

Thinking it couldn't be down to his academic skills.

'My Mam knows a bloke that works here, not sure who but he got me an interview and my charm did the rest' he smiled and winked at me.

'It'll be worth it all this you know, my dad reckons once you get a trade you can work anywhere Europe, America, Saudi', I told him watching his eyes light up.

'My brother Alan Emigrated to Australia Id love to go there' Colin said.

As we got to the office I looked up at the roof and thought shit I really don't like heights. I hunted round the area looking for a ladder then I spotted the old wooden set that John used lying next to a big green skip next to the dock. I picked up one end and Colin came over and grabbed the other end just as i spotted my dad coming off the gangway.

We lay the ladder against the roof and noticed my dad looking over from the dock with a pipe on his shoulder 'what you's up to?' He shouted over, me and Colin walked over and I explained about Dots hacksaw.

'Be careful up there' he said.

'Hey you know what this is by the way son?' He asked nudging his head to the heavy looking steel pipe on his shoulder.

'It's what's known as a spladunge pipe!' he stated.

'A what?' I asked,

Then he chucked the pipe over the fence into the water in the dock.

'Listen' he said with his hand on his ear!. There was a big splash!

'Did ya hear that! Spladunge!' he said laughing then walked off towards the plumbers shop.

I climbed up onto the ladder while Colin held the bottom steady for me while I nervously made it to the top.

I climbed over the ledge and up over onto the rooftop.

The sun was rising over the sea in the distance I stopped and admired the view for a minute and shouted down to Colin 'lovely view up here col!' then I spotted the hacksaw over where John repaired the guttering on the opposite side of the roof. There was a big puddle in the middle so I walked round the long way and picked up the hacksaw all rusty and wet.

'I bet that baldy prick left it up here on purpose' I thought to myself as I picked it up.

'Wow it is a good view up here' Colin said, 'what you doing up here man! who's footing the ladder now?' I looked at him shaking my head.

I started to head back over to the ladder but rather than walk round the puddle I decided to jump over it suddenly "CRASH!!". The roof gave in as I landed, I crashed through the roof falling completely through bouncing off an office desk and onto the floor of the office.

Colin looked down the hole shocked and seen me lying on the office floor in a heap covered in papers and bits off the roof.

'You alright?' He asked as I looked up in horror seeing what I'd done to the ceiling all the plaster was hanging down and a big gaping hole where I fell.

Paula the office secretary came running in she had only just arrived to work and hadn't even taken off her jacket yet and to her shock saw me come crashing through the roof.

'Are you ok she asked?' As she knelt down beside me giving me the once over.

'yeah I think so' I said sitting up as bits of plaster fell from my lap.

'What on earth were you doing up there?' She asked looking up to the gaping hole in the ceiling.

I explained the full story about the hacksaw and she looked on full of concern 'your gonna have to go to the first aid room make sure your ok' as she helped me up onto my feet.

Just then Colin popped his head through the hole 'it looks like it's gonna piss down out here!'.

I burst out laughing but I immediately stopped when I seen the look on Paula's face.

Paula told Colin to stay putt and not to move while she took me to the first aid room.

As we walked away from the office I noticed Dot was walking towards us with a scruffy looking bloke with a big red angry looking face and a massive beer belly sticking out of his overalls.

'Aright Paula' the big bloke grunted in a husky voice.

'Could you lads do me a favor and foot the ladder down there, one of the apprentices is up on the roof that Andy's just fell through'.

'Aye no bother pet!' the other bloke said and headed down towards the office.

'Cheers Duncan' Paula shouted.

Dot just stood there open mouthed looking at me.

I handed him his hacksaw and said 'sorry about that John left it on the roof' he burst out laughing 'just like your fatha!', he said and followed Duncan down towards the office.

Paula took me into a small room which looked a bit like my doctors surgery apart from it being a bit scruffy and white paint peeling off the walls.

Paula gave me the once over stating that the nurse didn't start till nine o'clock but she was a trained first aider herself.

After checking my blood pressure and shining a torch in my eyes and a few other checks she was happy to let me go, so I thanked her and apologized for the mess I'd made of her office.

'Don't worry I'll get Andy the joiner to fix the roof but this will have to go in the Accident book make sure you come back and see Gavin when he comes in' Okay' I replied walking out the door and heading for the bait hut.

As I walked in the cabin Iain was stood there with his Newcastle cup in one hand and a fag in the other he seen me covered in plaster looking in a bit of a state and burst out laughing 'what the hells happened now?'.

Just then the door burst open and John came storming over 'what's this you fell through the office roof?' The place erupted as the other apprentices all burst out laughing. He looked at Iain and took his fag out his mouth and dropped it in his coffee 'what have I told you about smoking in here?' He ranted 'And what's that smell of bloody fish?' He shouted with his nose in the air.

'You two follow me' he said grabbing mine and Iain's arms 'and the rest of you clean this shit hole up it bloody stinks!'.

As we got outside John noticed I didn't have my overalls on, 'oh for fucks sake! get in there and get ready' he screamed shoving me back towards the door. I got my gear on as quick as I could and joined John and Iain in the plumbing shop.

'What the hell were you doing on the roof ya lunatic?' John said angrily 'is there something wrong with you?' I tried to explain about Dots hacksaw but he just quickly dismissed what I said and started a new rant.

'Right the boat is going on sea trials tomorrow so we have loads of work on today, no more piss farting about! Iain your coming with me and Andrew your going to give Duncan a hand.' Iain looked devastated the thought of being stuck with that miserable git all day, I winked and give him a sly grin when john's back was turned.

Shortly after Duncan came storming in ranting and raving how the pipes are rotten,

'They should be all ripped out and started again' he shouted and threw a pipe in temper across the floor,

'I've been here since 5 o'clock this bastard morning' he screamed.

'Aright, Dunc calm down, the boy here is gonna give you a hand' John shouted back

'Well I hope he's got a magic wand!' Duncan said

Giving me a filthy look.

Iain looked over and smirked, looks like I got the short straw again I thought!.

Iain and John walked out the shop and left me alone with this angry scary bloke.

He started going through the pipe rack throwing bits of pipe around in a rage.

'Grab hold of that he shouted at me' pointing to a length of pipe hanging in the rack I tried pulling at the pipe but it wouldn't budge!. Duncan came over and shouted in my face 'Grab hold of it man!' His breath stank of booze and his red face looked even redder close up and his eyes were bulging! this man looked like a serious drinker and a very scary bloke.

He shoved me out the way and grabbed the pipe and pulled it out the rack and threw it effortlessly on the steel bench cursing and swearing as he did so.

Dot came walking in and was smirking as I stood there gob smacked while Duncan grabbed the pipe slamming it into what looked like a pipe bending machine throwing bits of pipe about in a tantrum.

Dot whispered in my ear

'Don't wind him up he's a bloody lunatic, Duncan disorderly they call him' he said smirking.

I'd already gathered as much as I tried helping him but he just lost his temper and swore at me.

He eventually got the bending machine working and was pumping on a handle making the pipe bend.

'Pump that till I tell you to stop' Duncan shouted I did as I was told and kept pushing on this handle while Duncan looked on 'right stop!' I stopped and Duncan grabbed the pipe out of the machine and threw it on the bench with a big crash and bang.

He started measuring the pipe and made two black marks on each end of the pipe with his marker pen and shouted at me 'cut there and there' pointing to the marks he'd just made and stormed out leaving me looking at Dot puzzled.

Dot laughed and gave me a hand lifting the pipe into the saw and showed me how to work it, he gripped the pipe in the machine vice. He pressed the green button and the machine began

cutting the pipe.
'Cheers Dot' I said grateful for his help
'If I didn't he'd only go off on one! he's like a spoilt little kid drunken Duncan, right bad tempered bastard' Dot said.
My day just gets worse I thought as I undid the vice and turned the pipe round to cut the other end. Dot gripped the vice and told me to press the green button which I did and the saw started cutting the pipe.

Duncan came back in seeing the pipe in the saw seemed to calm him down a bit.
He went over to a big wooden box in the corner looking for something and shouted to Dot 'where's all the fucking flanges?' Dot said I'll go and get you a couple! do you want me to weld them on for ya?'
'Aye please mate' Duncan said sounding like a normal person again.

After a few minutes Dot came back with two metal disks with holes in them and placed them on the bench he grabbed a grinder and cleaned the paint off each end of the pipe and explained to me what he was doing as he pulled out his spirit level and put the flanges on the pipe two holes square.
He then put on a welding screen on and shouted "eyes!" I didn't know what he was on about till he sparked up the welding machine almost blinding me.
Duncan looked on laughing shouting 'he said eyes! Cover your eyes you idiot'.
He shook his head and got the level and placed it on the flange and said to dot 'ok mate' again Dot shouted 'Eyes' this time I covered my eyes as he welded the flange to the pipe then dot flipped the pipe round and did the same again.
A few minutes later Dot had finished and cooled the pipe down in a big tin container full of water.
Duncan told me to grab the pipe as he headed out the pipe shop towards the ship with his tool bag.
'Ya welcome Dunc!' Dot shouted sarcastically as I followed Duncan out the shop with the pipe on my shoulder.
As I walked out the door the pipe seemed to get heavier on my shoulder I tried to keep up with Duncan but couldn't I had to stop to rest.
After a minute or so I lifted the pipe onto my other shoulder and continued walking towards the ship I stopped at the gangway and swapped shoulders again and walked on board I looked around and Duncan was nowhere to be seen. Iain came out of a door to my left I asked him if he'd seen Drunken Duncan he said "aye is that the pisshead who looks like he's heads gonna explode?'.
That's him I explained and told him what a nutcase he is.
'He's over there look!' Iain said laughing as Duncan was in a tantrum throwing rubbish bags and old pipes 'look at the state of this place man!' He screamed from the hanger.
I wandered over and Duncan pointed to the space where the pipe was going we just made.
'If this doesn't fit I'm away!' he shouted as he grabbed the pipe off my shoulder.
'Give me the bolts and gaskets' he shouted
'what bolts and gaskets?' I asked.

Duncan went into a rage screaming I was supposed to pick the bag up off the bench,
'You never told me too' I replied immediately regretting it.He looked at me and said 'go and get them now!' with an evil look on his face.
I ran as quick as I could up to the plumber shop but Gavin stopped me 'Mr Carter! come with me' he shouted
'I can't, drunken Duncan..' I tried to blurt out the words but he grabbed me and pulled me towards the office.
He told me to sit down while he pulled out a letter and passed it to me. Before I had a chance to read it he said 'I'm issuing you with a written warning' I couldn't believe it I was gutted, only my first week and I was getting a warning.
'Gavin I'm sorry it was an accident I was just trying to get Dots hacksaw back'.
'You disregarded safety Andrew that's the main issue here'.
Gavin explained how I could have been killed and this hasn't been the only incident.
I just kept quiet thinking John must have opened his mouth.

After about ten minutes of filling in forms I was free to head back to work.
I headed to the plumbers shop and seen Duncan grab a bag off the bench.
'Where the hell have you been?' He screamed at me.
'I got dragged into the office!' I tried to explain but he was in one of his tantrums throwing things about and not listening to me.
He grabbed the bag of bolts and gaskets and stormed out so I followed him almost running to catch him up.
'I'm sorry, Gavin dragged me in the office and gave me a written warning' I said trying to calm things down.
'You deserve a warning your useless like your dad'. I was close to losing it myself now, I stopped for a second tried to calm myself down I took a deep breath then followed the dickhead on board.

Back on board Duncan told me to grab one end of the pipe as he grabbed the other we tried it in the space the old pipe came out of but even I could see the pipe wasn't the right angle and looked way to short.
But Duncan insisted it would fit we struggled to get the pipe to fit for about five minutes when suddenly Duncan grabbed the pipe and threw it across the hanger smashing against an electrical box that cracked and a big chunk fell off 'that's it fuck it I've had enough!' he screamed and walked out.
I walked to the hanger door and seen him wandering off the gangway to the dockside and kicking a bin at the bottom of the gangway over in a rage.
I stood there wondering what to do next when Decka crept up on me and gave me the shock of my life when he made a scream sound in my ear.
'Your jumpy aren't ya' Decka chuckled.
I explained the day I'd had the roof, the tantrums of Duncan the warning, he just laughed 'I'm on my third written warning man!
they give them out for no reason here man!'.
He explained how he drove a forklift truck into the river while him and the lads were messing

about.

'Hey man you'd have to kill someone to get sacked from here' he laughed.
'Some of the dickheads here I just might'
I replied.

Dinner time finally arrived I headed into the bait cabin with Decka soon as we walked in we noticed the smell of rotten fish was getting stronger 'that honks!' Decka shouted as he sat down next to Iain who was arm wrestling Dan.
'Get in!' Iain shouts as he slams Dan's hand down on the table 'next' he shouts I jump opposite him. Before we start Decka explains my arm is in the wrong position he straightened up my arm then we started.
Within seconds my arm has been slammed down I was beaten easily.

I sit down next to Dan as Decka takes the position in front of Iain to take him on.
'Where's Colin?' I asked Dan.
'He's gone home for dinner, he only lives up the road' Dan explained.

Iain jumped up celebrating as he beat a gob smacked Decka.
Five minutes later Colin came limping through the door black and blue and blood pouring from his nose.
'Bloody hell Col you ok?' Dan asked. Everyone rushed over to see if he was ok.
"You should see the other bloke" he laughed as he winced in pain holding his ribs.
Colin sat down Decka handed him a bottle of water and told Dan to get some bog roll.
'Who did this to you?' Decka asked
'Nobody' Colin said and looked at me.
Decka noticed him looking at me and said 'Haway il take you to see the nurse' and walked him outside.
'Bloody hell who'd do that! he wouldn't hurt a fly Colin!'
Dan shouted.
Everyone just sat in silence wondering what had happened but I knew and I was raging.
I kept quiet keeping Colin's promise but I was a bit unsure what to do for the best.

John came bursting through the door and grabbed me by the ear and shouted of ian to get his finger out.
He dragged me to the plumbers shop and started ranting 'what the hell happened with Duncan disorderly? he's packed his tools and gone'.
'Nothing to do with me the blokes a lunatic'. I explained what had happened.
Dot came in and caught half the story and joined in the conversation 'he's off his head man! He couldn't fit a pipe in a snowman's mouth. All he's bothered about is drink!' John listening to Dot and had to agree.
'Look Dot take the lad here and fit that pipe will ya? Remake it whatever you have to do bud'.
John walked out leaving me with Dot.
I wasn't listening as Dot rambled on about the pipe and what we were going to do, my thoughts were with Colin.

There must be something I could do I thought.

My thoughts were broken by Decka who said to me 'word outside now!'.

I wandered outside while Dot nodded that it was ok.

Soon as I got outside Decka had his nose right in my face with a scary look on his face.

'Has this got something to do with you? I seen the way Colin looked at you' Decka shouted.

'No no honest but..'

'But what?' Decka interrupted you better start talking!'

I explained to Decka that I'd made a promise to Colin that I wouldn't say anything but I could see from the look in his eyes he wasn't going anywhere till I told him so I explained everything.

'Any idea where he lives?' Decka asked

'No idea, Dan reckons he lives locally like!' I replied.

Dot headed out of the plumbers shop.

I explained to Decka I better go and I quickly ran to catch up with Dot who was heading towards the ship.

I caught up with Dot near the crane just as Gavin was walking towards us with Colin all battered and bruised holding his ribs.

They walked off towards the bait hut.

'They must be sending him home' I said to Dot.

But his face looked full of concern 'what's happened?' Dot screamed looking at me

'Don't know' I said but he looked at me sensing I wasn't telling the truth

'You'd better start talking' Dot said grabbing my overalls and pinning me up against the wall with a look of rage on his face.

I was shocked but told him what I knew and that I'd told Decka after promising Colin I wouldn't.

Dot ran towards the plumbers shop and shouted of Decka within a couple of minutes Decka and Dot came running out the shop and quickly jumped in Deckas saxo.

Decka sped away but quickly spun the car round when he saw me and pulled up next to me.

'Get in!' Decka shouted.

I quickly jumped in the back seat and we sped off towards the gate.

'Where we going?' I asked

Decka looked in his mirror and said

'To pay somebody a little visit'.

A few minutes later we skidded to a stop outside a scruffy looking block of flats.

'Which way Dot?' Decka shouted,

'Up There number 44' Dot said pointing up to the fourth level. Decka charged up the concrete steps with me and Dot following trying to keep up.

'Smells worse than the bait cabin in here' I commented as the stairwell stank of stale piss.

We got to the fourth floor and Dot said 'hang on Decka let me, he might not even be in'.

Decka stepped aside and let dot knock on the big blue door with a crack in the frosted glass window.

A couple of seconds later the door opened and a small chubby dark haired woman in her mid forties opened the door with the biggest black eye I'd ever seen.

'What the hell are you doing here?' the woman screamed at Dot.
'Have you looked in the mirror? and Colin's in a worse state than Russia!'
The woman replied 'look you gave up your right to care when you pissed off all those years ago, we don't need you!'.
Dot stood staring at her in disbelief
'Pam, Look at the state of you man!, where's that drunken prick?' Dot asked.
Decka suddenly without warning went storming past Pam and headed into the flat. Suddenly we heard a big crash and bang and then shouting and screaming then before we knew it Decka came through the door with a battered looking Duncan disorderly.
I looked at Dot stunned as Decka had the heavy built bloke by the throat and dragged him to the railing that looked down onto where we parked the car four stories down.
Decka had Duncan by the throat leaning him over the balcony with Duncan now pleading for his life and Pam screaming.

'You listen carefully Duncan' Decka had his nose in Duncan's face staring into his eyes shouting 'you leave here now and if you ever show your face round here again, your going head first over there, you hear me?'.

Duncan screamed in tears 'yes, yes please just let me go!' Decka pulled him away from the balcony and slammed him against the wall next to the door then head butted him in the nose.
Duncan fell to the floor clutching his bloodied nose and
Pam screamed 'enough!' and grabbed Decka who was about to kick Duncan while he was on the floor.
Pam shouted at Duncan 'just get your things and go please!'
Tears streaming down her face.
Decka picked him up off the floor and shoved him towards the front door, he quickly scrambled to his feet and staggered in the house doing as he was told.
Colin appeared from the stairwell and went running to his Mam and hugged her 'you ok Mam? What's happening?' he asked
'It's ok son it's all going to be ok now' she hugged him and kissed him on the forehead.

A few minutes later Duncan came staggering out the house with a tatty old brown suitcase and a big bag of tools.
Decka grabbed the tool bag and threw it over the balcony then suddenly heard a big crash and a car alarm going off.
"Bollocks!" Decka screamed as he looked over the balcony and realized the tool bag had just smashed through his windscreen of his pride and joy.
Duncan seen the angry look on Decka's face and ran as fast as he could clutching his and ribs and headed down the stairwell out of sight.
I shouted after him 'you've forgot ya case!' and threw it over the balcony with another big crash!
Suddenly Decka looked at me and this time I started running for the stairwell, but Decka just looked at Dot and the two of them burst out laughing.

Colin and his Mam headed inside and Pam turned and looked at Decka and Dot and gave a

smile
'Thanks lads'.

Chapter 6
Last laughs and photographs.

For once I woke up early even shouted of my Dad to get up out of bed!.
The only reply I got was 'piss off!'.

I sat waiting in the car very bored so I ejected my cassette out of my Walkman and stuck it in the car cassette player.

My dad jumped in the driver seat eventually and said 'you shit the bed?
Not like you to be up at this time!'.

As he turned out of the square my cassette came on and corner shops Brimful of asha started playing.
I sat waiting for him to say something seems as though I was always criticizing his choice in music.

A minute or so later the rant came just as my dad pulled over at the bus stop and Dicky jumped in the back.
'What's this shit? Everybody needs a bosom for a pillow?'
Dicky also joined in 'it's all boy band shite now fawlty! no taste in music the kids of today!'. The verve bittersweet symphony came on next and not a word between them. My dad even hummed along at one point.
I sat there looking all smug knowing that song won them over,
then the next track came on.."Aqua, Barbie girl" my dad ejected the tape and threw it out the window and looked at me in disgust!. He then raked about in his side door while keeping one eye on the road and eventually found what he was looking for. He popped in the cassette and Johnny cash ring of fire came on 'that's more like it fawlty' Dicky shouted as I sat there sulking.

As we pulled into the to car park at the dockyard JJ was walking past he stopped and looked at us in shock, rubbing his eyes and started clapping his hands
'on time for once?' He shouted as we got out the car then started laughing to himself as he walked down towards the plumbers shop.
My dad and Dickie headed down to there locker room as
I walked over towards the bait hut.

I noticed Ricky heading in the door before me 'alright mate, welcome back' I said patting him on the back.
'Bloody hell it stinks in here!' he said as he headed in towards his locker.
I sat down opposite Colin next to Iain
'Good thing he got over that bad case of Pringles eh Colin!' Iain laughed.
Ricky kicked off his trainers and popped on his overalls then slipped his foot into his left rigger boot as we all looked on in anticipation knowing Iain had stuffed a fish in his right rigger boot the other day.

Ricky stopped what he was doing then looked round at Iain "pringles?" He said looking puzzled. He then carried on and popped his right foot in his boot and there was a crunchy squishy sound accompanied by a horrendous smell of rotten fish.

Ricky started reaching to be sick as he pulled his foot out the boot and seen what remained of the fish, He ran to the door with his hand over his mouth and quickly opened the door and vomited,

he looked up in horror to see John stood there now with puke all over his white overalls.

We all howled with laughter as Ricky was dragged out the cabin by his ear.

Ten minutes later John came back in wearing a new pair of overalls looking well pissed off. 'Right Dumb and Dumber!' he shouted 'your going to do your NVQs today you have to meet Davey Chocolate at the induction office in ten minutes' and stormed out slamming the door behind him.

'Davey Chocolate?' I said looking at Ian wondering if the name was a windup.

Ricky came bursting back in five minutes later rubbing his hands together grinning from ear to ear! 'get in! They've just said they're sending me home on full pay!' he laughed.

'After seeing me vomiting they think I'm still bad'. Dan shouted from the other table 'your gonna miss the crane game final'

'The what?' Iain asked.

Dan explained how there's a overhead crane in the big shed you have to grab the hook and someone lifts you up using the controller till your bottle goes and you shout stop, they then bring you back down.

'It's the final today between Colin and whoppa nappa!'.

'Who's whoppa Nappa?' I asked laughing.

'You know man! Gaz that Sparky with the massive head!'

'Who snipers dream?' Ian shouted

'Aye that's him, anyway he beat me yesterday and I got about six metres up, fearless he is, mind you Colin beat fat Kev so it'll them two in the final! it'll be some match like!' Dan explained.

'we have to go do our NVQs with Davey chocolate! Hopefully we don't miss it' I replied wondering if I should have a go myself.

Ten minutes later me and Iain were sat in the induction room playing coin football waiting for Davey whoever he was.

Just as I was celebrating my two nil lead the door opened and a huge guy well over six foot came in dressed in a smart pinstripe suit he was a strange looking bloke in his forties with jet black hair and a big pointy nose and a massive beer belly.

'Hello boys my names David Rowntree I'm the yards NVQ manager I'm here with you every Friday to help you do your books' he said in a very camp voice.

He explained how every week we had to keep a diary of our pipework we have done and we were to take pictures using the company camera.

'This week One of you will have the camera next week the other, right! Which one of you is

Andrew?' he asked, seeing me with my hand up he handed me the camera.
It was an old silver rectangular Kodak camera similar to the one my dad had at home.
'It's already got the film in all you have to do is take the pictures and give it back to me next Friday and il get them developed and get a new film put in for lain' Davey said showing me how to work the camera.

David seemed a nice guy and offered us tea and coffee and just sat chatting to us asking how work was so far and even came outside for a smoke with us smoking his old wooden pipe. He seemed very laid back he even gave lain a smoke of his pipe as he kept pestering him for a go and asking what it was like.
Back in the induction room he gave us both a big blue folder with about 300 empty pages.
'These folders will be full in three years from now, I want you to put in each job you do and a little description and a photo or sketch with each job'
Said Dave handing us information packs and a few forms to fill in.
After about thirty minutes or so he told us we could get back to work so we started heading out the door Dave handed me the camera which I'd totally forgot about leaving it on the table.
'Please be careful with the camera lads it's the only one they've given me and use it wisely!'
Dave said before heading off to his maroon Rover parked outside the office.

We were just about to head to the plumbers shop when lain suddenly remembered the crane game final.
We quickly ran past the plumbers shop door hoping John wasn't in there and headed into the big shed. As we ran through the door i tripped again over the same bottom part of the bastard door frame that got me the other day and I fell to the ground to roars of laughter from the lads standing round the toolboxes.
lain picked up the camera that fell out of my hand and ran in front of me and took a picture as I struggled to get to my feet.

Dot and my dad and a few others stood laughing as I got to my feet, luckily today there wasn't a big puddle of oil so I just dusted myself down shook my head and headed over to the crane where Dan and a few others where preparing for the big finale.

We had missed Colin's attempt but it was a very respectable ten meters up Dan informed us.
Now was Gary's turn, or whoppa knappa as the lads call him.
My god I thought he did have a big head, he was tall and average build but he had a massive head that wasn't really in proportion with the rest of his body.
Gaz cracked his knuckles then reached up and grabbed the crane hook as Dan pressed the up bottom on the controls and he began to move up slowly one meter then two he continued going up with nothing to cushion his fall if he fell, I stood rooted to the spot watching open mouthed as whoppa nappa showed no fear and smashed Colin's record. Dan announced 'I reckon twelve meters well done Gaz' he shouted up and started bringing him down.
When his feet finally touched the ground safely I breathed a sigh of relief.
Everyone shouted well done whistled and patted him on the back as he walked by arms raiser in triumph.

'Well done whoppa nappa' I shouted as he walked past

'You what? Dickhead!' He shouted over to me and had a look in his eye like he was going to whack me but he just walked over to dot and my dad and the rest and shook his head.

Dan looked at me stunned

and informed me people don't normally say that to his face.


As all the other apprentices left it was only me and Iain.

I was feeling brave and my competitive side was beating my fear of heights.

'Haway let's give it a shot' I said walking over to the hook.

Iain grabbed the controller that hung down on a thick black cable

'Ready' Iain shouted

'Aye' as I grabbed the hook and off I went heading upwards, soon as I got about a meter up I started panicking but Iain just kept pushing the up button and eventually stopped about five meters up and then took my picture with the camera.

Whoppa napper came running over and snatched the controller 'whoppa napper eh!' He shouted and started moving the crane towards the back of the shed with me clinging on screaming 'stop' he kept going I was finding it hard to keep grip as the crane bumped along and I'd started swinging and swaying,

he finally started slowing down as my dad shouted over

'Hey man be careful!' Whoppa nappa noticed my dad was pissed off so he lowered me down a little bit to a safer height and Maneuvered me over the cooling tank.

The cooling tank was basically a big steel tank the sheet metal workers used.

it was full of water to cool hot metals down.

I looked down below me there was only a meter drop then another meter or so of dirty rusty coloured water,

whoppa nappa left me to hang above the water and walked away laughing handing the controller to Iain. My dad came over as Iain began taking more pictures with his free hand.

'Haway!' my dad said "give me the controller" and grabbed it off Iain and was just about to maneuver me away from the water but my arms were aching and my fingers were starting to slip down the hook. Soon as my dad got the crane moving I couldn't hold on any longer and my fingers started slipping and I fell! there was a massive splash as I fell feet first into the water up to my waist then fell backwards fully submerging myself into the rusty smelly water.

I was drenched the water felt freezing Cold and my overalls and wet clothes felt so heavy as they clung to my skin.

I quickly scrambled to my feet and climbed up onto the edge of the tank and jumped out.

Sounds of hysterical laughter came from my dad and Iain and the others as I Climbed up off the floor and stood there soaked through to my skin. Iain began again taking pictures of me stood there freezing and drenched.


Back at the bait room for dinner time I'd took all my wet clothes off and jumped into Ricky's spare pair of overalls which were about three sizes too small and looked ridiculously tight. I hung my wet clothes over various chairs and turned the electric heaters on full blast to try and dry them out.

'it's like a sauna in here!' Dan shouted as he burst through the door.

I just ignored him as I was too busy trying to hang my soaking wet boxer shorts next to my wet socks on the top of the door of my locker.

Iain burst in the door and started laughing seeing all my wet clothes hanging round the place.
'Good thing I had the camera!' he shouted.
'Look man Davey is going to go mad that's supposed to be for my work'
I snapped at Iain.
'Look it's no bother we will get your mate whoppa nappa to delete the pictures he's a sparky isn't he? He'll know how to do it then we can take some pictures of pipes in the plumbers shop, there's loads of pipes in there we can just pretend you made them' Iain said.
'Good thinking batman!' Dan shouted
'Thank you robin!' Iain replied with a wink and a nod.
It's worth a try I suppose and it will give me a chance to apologize I thought.

After about ten minutes of rooting around old lockers to find some old boots I used Ricky's left rigger boot and a random right boot that didn't match and had laces unlike my left.

We headed over to the electricians place which was situated just opposite the plumbers shop so we ran hoping John wouldn't see us.

We opened the big wooden door with a sign on that said 'keep out skilled tradesman only'
We walked into the stuffy little shed there were coils of cables hung up everywhere and four scruffy looking blokes sitting on a wooden bench drinking tea one of them was whoppa napper who looked at me with an angry glare.
Iain passed me the camera and nudged me forward.
'Sorry to bother you lads, just wondering if any of you's know anything about cameras?'
I asked nervously.
I explained the situation and told him there were pictures on there that needed deleting I said as whopper napper took the camera from me.
'And I'm very sorry about earlier' I said as I watched him giving it the once over.
'There's nothing you can do once you've took the pictures but you still have twenty left' he explained. 'Don't know why your so bothered! Davey is sound anyway he'll probably just laugh about it,
just take some random pictures of pipes on the boat and pretend you made them'
Whoppa said to which I replied 'good thinking batman' for some god knowing reason.
'Did you just call me fat man?' He screamed and stood up
'No,No I said Batman' I replied nervously.
'Batman? why the fuck did you just call me batman?' He asked as I stood there cringing! I looked over at Iain he was hiding his face in an embarrassing cringe stricken way.
'You were supposed to say thank you robin.. ' I stuttered struggling to get my words out
'Should I have? Sorry'
He said obviously being sarcastic.
I stood there cheeks now glowing red with embarrassment as the four blokes looked at me like I was some sort of weirdo as I stood there with odd boots and naked under my skin tight overalls.

I just quickly snatched the camera and ran out the door.

Iain followed me out and looked at me and just burst out laughing. 'That was the most horrible cringe worthy moment I've ever seen' he said with tears streaming down his face with laughter.

We headed back to the plumbers shop where John stood with his hands on his hips 'where the hell have you two been?' He screamed.

'Taking pictures of our work' I said showing him the camera.

'What work? You've done no work!' He shouted.

'It's a shame you didn't have the camera earlier in the week, you could have took a picture of the floods you caused or even the big hole in the office roof you fell through' John shouted staring at me with a confused look, probably wondering why I was wearing odd boots and had no clothes on under my overalls.

'Anyway there's a toolbox talk in the big shed at two o'clock this afternoon so be there! It's pointless giving you a job now just wait here and try not to break anything or flood the place!' he shouted as he stormed out the door passing Decka on his way in 'aright ladies, you got the camera this week young fawlty?' Decka said noticing the camera in my hand.

I explained all the pictures Iain took he laughed and said 'hey just do what I did! watch this!', he said picking up a pipe with a flange on one end and got his spirit level out and popped it on the top. He gave Iain the camera and directed me where to stand holding the spirit level over the bolt holes of the flange and stepped behind me out of my view 'left arm up a bit' he shouted from behind me and told Iain to take the picture.

I didn't realize he was behind me undoing his pants and bending over showing his arse as Iain took the picture.

Then he guided me to a pipe which had been completed by someone else he then turned away from me briefly then handed me the pipe and told me to stand holding it to the camera.

I should have realized something was going on when Iain started smirking but I happily posed for the picture,

written in black marker on the side of the pipe facing the camera was "I have a tiny penis" which I didn't see.

Then he guided me to the welding machine and switched it on and gave me a welding mask to put on and grabbed the pipe with the flange on and put it on the workbench.

'Right get ready to weld just bend over and tap it on the pipe and it will spark up and look like your welding and Iain you take the picture' he shouted to Iain as I leaned over the table sparking the torch to life not realizing Decka was posing as if he had me bent over the table.

'There you go there's three jobs you've done now, Davey will be ok about the other pictures man! He's a good bloke chocolate'. Decka said putting my mind at rest.

'Aye he's sound even let me smoke his pipe' Iain replied as me and Decka grinned.

'Aye I bet he did' laughed Decka.

'Cheers for this' I said thinking again this lad had saved the day.

'Haway lads it's two o clock toolbox talk' he said looking at his watch and quickly darting out the door.

'What's a toolbox talk?' I asked Iain

He opened the lid of a toolbox on the bench and muttered 'hello I'm a toolbox' in a squeaky voice lifting the lid up and down as he spoke.

Me and Iain eventually walked into the big shed and the meeting was already under way and about a hundred blokes were gathered round Gavin, Paula and photo Finish and some other bloke I'd never seen before.
Everybody turned to look at me as I followed Iain in as the wind suddenly picked up and slammed the big metal door behind me with a massive bang.
There I was stood with odd boots and clearly naked under my overalls.
There were a few odd looks and a few scattered laughs as I stood there red faced wanting the ground to swallow me up.
'Thanks for that entrance lads' Gavin shouted with an angry look on his face.
Then the other bloke looked at me in a strange way then began shouting
'As I was saying until I was rudely interrupted, we have no more work on the order books here unfortunately, as soon as the orange leaf goes we will have to let a lot of you go, but the Hepburn yard has a requirement for a few trades so if that interests any of you please sign the sheet that is being passed around and make a note next to your name that you're interested and we will contact you in due course, now again lads I'd like to take this opportunity to thank you for all your hard work and I assure you all soon as work picks up here we will be in touch'.
'So when we getting our notice?' One of the platers at the back shouted.
'Paula here has a some letters for a lot of you,
again I'm sorry' the bloke shouted holding his hand up apologetically.

Me and Iain headed back to the bait room a little shocked at what we just heard.
The other apprentices were sat round wondering where that left us.

After about ten minutes or so Gavin came in and informed us all we were all being transferred to the Hepburn yard on Monday to continue our apprenticeships there as it was going to be a while before another ship came in.
'Take the rest of the afternoon off lads to make arrangements to get there on Monday and here is the full address and all information needed' he said as he handed us all a little handbook.
'Take this opportunity as a fresh start lads and no more mucking about' he shouted as he walked out slamming the door.
We all stripped off our overalls ready to leave.
I hid behind the locker door as I had nothing underneath.
I reached over to get my overalls from the top of the heater when suddenly Iain slammed my locker door shut and started taking pictures of me naked 'ow man!' I shouted quickly pulling my boxer shorts on. I grabbed the camera and suddenly the door opened and photo finish popped his head in.
'Il need that camera back Andrew it's property of Wear dock' Gavin said snatching the camera from me 'don't worry I'll get the film to David he said after seeing the worried expression on my face.
'Cheers' I replied as Iain burst out laughing.

My dad popped his head in the bait room just as Gavin left and said 'we are all off to boozer if you fancy it lads!, a nice farewell drink seems as though the bastards have laid us off, you's coming?'.

Most of the lads agreed and we arranged to meet in 'cheers' a pub about half a mile up the bank.

Myself, Iain, Dan and Colin stuffed our overalls and boots into the back of my dads car and we all squeezed in the back seat with my dad and Dickie singing along to Johnny cash ring of fire again!.

My dad mounted the curb right outside the pub door and we all climbed out.

'I wouldn't leave ya car there fawlty, it'll get nicked round here'

Dicky warned my Dad.

'Ya having a laugh aren't you, who'd want to nick that?' I shouted as we all walked into the pub and my dad slapped me on the back of the head.

My dad pulled out his wallet and said 'I'll get this round in lads' just as blue peter and Decka walked through the door 'good man fawlty' Decka shouted 'eight pints of lager please pet' my dad shouted over to the rough looking blonde busty barmaid wiping down the bar with a cloth.

Peter sat on the stool next to my dad ogling as the barmaid began pouring the drinks.

she noticed him staring and shouted over 'having a good look there blue?' Not phased at all blue replied 'I bet you a fiver I can make your tits move without touching them Lil' she stopped pouring the drinks and walked over to blue with her hands on her hips 'you what?'

'I'm serious I bet you five pound I can make your tits move without even touching them'

Peter replied slamming a five pound note on the bar.

She looked at him curiously and picked up the fiver to see if it was real and threw it back on the bar.

'You reckon you can make my tits move without touching them? and you'll give me a fiver if you can't?' she said looking at blue nodding.

'Okay then your on' she said standing there looking confused.

Peter stood up started rubbing his forehead with his thumbs making a quiet humming noise as we all looked on.

He suddenly reached across the bar grabbed her breasts and squeezed them and moved them up and down as everyone looked on shocked.

'Best fiver I've ever spent' he shouted handing her the five pound note.

'You cheeky Bastard!' she screamed throwing half a pint of lager at him while laughing her head off as peter scarpered towards the pool table.

My dad paid for the drinks handing her a twenty pound note telling her to keep the change.

Lil could see him struggling to carry four of the beers to a table opposite the bar.

'Do you want a tray?' Lil asked

'Do you not think I've got enough to carry?' My dad replied as he carried the other four and plonked them on the table.

The eight of us were getting ready to play killer pool as blue explained the rules which were:

Each player was given one life,
We take turns and if you pot a ball you stay in and if you miss you lose your life and your out.
We each pay a pound and the winner (the last one with a life left) wins the money. The first person to lose a life must do a forfeit which the winner decides.
If the loser doesn't do the forfeit he has been given he has to buy every player a drink of their choice.
We all agreed to the rules and put a pound in an empty pint glass that sat on the edge of the pool table.

A few other lads came through the doors and blue asked if they wanted to join in.
'Na your alright mate I'm not running round naked again like last time!'
Fat kev shouted over.
My heart sank it sounded like these forfeits get pretty extreme and I was hopeless at pool I thought.
'No silly dares or your all out!' Lil the barmaid shouted over at blue.
'This is a respectable pub no one wants to see fat naked men in their fifties running about again!' lil yelled pointing at fat kev.
'Hey it's not a brick in there ya know lil! I've got feelings.'
Kev snapped back pointing to his chest giving lil a wink.

A couple of the other lads that came in and joined the game and blue wrote their names on the blackboard by the dartboard.

First up was me as Zack the welder come up with the idea that alphabetical order was the fairest way to go.
I was feeling quite confident as I broke off and potted two balls but what I didn't see was the white ball roll into the top right pocket.
'Bollocks!'
I shouted.
'Right that's young fawlty first one out, the winner decides his dare' blue shouted rubbing my name out written in chalk on the blackboard.

I could only watch and hope somebody sensible won like my dad or Dan,
god help me if Billy Animal or Blue won I thought.

It was a tense game.
Colin missed a really easy black that lay over the pocket his name was also scrubbed off the chalkboard.
Dan missed a tricky blue spot undercutting it so it only just missed the middle pocket.
My dad miscued and didn't even hit a ball he was also out.
As the game went on more lads missed and dropped out and soon there was only two left.
Iain was facing Billy animal in the final as I looked on in horror.
Billy had a tricky shot as the white was tight up against the top cushion and the only two balls left to pot were two spotted balls both sitting in the middle of the table touching each other.

Billy stared at the table thinking of his next move while scratching his chin eying up his options.
'I'm just gonna have to blast them' he said looking very serious.
He squatted down and carefully prepared to take his shot.
Suddenly he stopped and said to Iain 'right fancy a wager? I bet you all the money in the jar I can hit every cushion kiss that ball on the left and drop the other ball in the middle bag' Iain looked on confused thinking Steve Davis couldn't pull that shot off.
'So I get eighteen quid?'
Iain replied
'Only if I don't do it, but if I do I win the game and win the eight quid in the pot!'.
Iain looked at the balls on the table and looked at Billy and agreed.
They shook hands on it and Billy squatted down again ready to take his shot as we all looked on in anticipation thinking surely this can't be done.
Billy moved the cue back and forwards as everyone watched in silence.
Suddenly he stood up threw the cue to the floor ran round the table punched every cushion then reached over picked up one of the balls off the table held it to his lips kissed it then picked the other ball up and dropped it in the middle pocket.
'There ya go son' Billy shouted then poured all the pound coins out of the pint glass into his hand as everyone looked on and howled with laughter while Iain just stood there open mouthed.

Iain eventually seen the funny side and me and him sat giggling as my fate was being decided by Billy and the rest of the lads still crowded round the pool table.
Billy eventually came over and said 'right son! with it being the first dare we're gonna go easy on you!, all you have to do is go over to that bus stop over the road there' he said pointing to a bus stop out the window with about six people all stood there waiting for the bus. 'You have to go over and just lie down on the ground and not say a word for five minutes' if you talk to anyone you lose and you have to buy everyone a drink'.

It didn't seem too bad I thought at least it didn't involve getting naked and it's not like I had a choice I only had about a fiver left in my pocket so I reluctantly agreed and headed out the door as everyone crowded round the window to witness my dare.

I had hoped the bus would have came by the time I'd crossed the road but there was no sign of it only more people at the bus stop.
There was now about a dozen or so people standing there.
I glanced at my watch and to everyone's amazement I walked into the bus shelter and lay down on the ground and crossed my legs and put my hands behind my head.
A couple of teenage girls laughed and whispered to each other as I tried to ignore them and just stared at the bus shelter roof.
A little old lady wandered over asked me if I was ok to which I nodded. She sat back down looking puzzled.
A dark haired woman moved her pram so she could see my face and said 'are you okay son?'
Again I replied nodding.
Then out of nowhere Whoppa Nappa appeared and knelt down next to me 'you alright?' I gave him a nod and a smile and he looked at me with a very strange look and said 'are you on

drugs?' I shook my head and looked at my watch.

Still four more minutes to go.

Whoppa nappa explained to everyone that I work at the dockyard and that I've been acting weird all day and said I must be on something.

Suddenly a bus pulled up and everyone got on except Whoppa nappa who kept asking me questions like how many fingers am I holding up? Then the bus driver got out of his booth and got off the bus to see what was happening and he Knelt down next to me saying 'are you okay son?'

I nodded again.

'Maybe we should take him to the hospital' the driver said 'I go past the general'.

I shook my head to the driver but he looked at whopper nappa and said 'come on let's get the lad up'. The driver and whoppa nappa tried to get me to my feet but I wriggled about not letting them pick me up eventually I gave up and screamed 'it's a dare!' and pointed over to the pub window where there was about twenty faces pressed against the window laughing their heads off.

'And now you owe everyone a drink!' Whoppa nappa shouted with arms raised and ran over the road into the pub.'prick' I shouted after him realizing he must have been in the bar and knew what was going to happen if I spoke. I looked at my watch thinking surely I've gone over five minutes but it was still only three minutes gone.

The bus driver stepped away from me and jumped back on the bus and called me an idiot and drove off as I got back to my feet and headed over to the pub.

There was a big cheer as I walked into the bar and a crowd of people shouting what drinks they wanted.

I felt cheated I would have done it without speaking easily had Whoppa nappa not turned up.

I borrowed twenty quid off my dad and went to the bar to get the drinks in.

I slumped over the bar and waved the twenty pound note to lil who came over. I looked over to my left and

Billy Animal was sat on the bar stool next to me he grabbed my hand and winked 'put your money away son I'm getting these in'

the look on his face said it all he smiled and told me he wouldn't let an apprentice pay for the drinks and patted me on the back.

'Your a good kid just like ya fatha! Just enjoy yourself and don't stress about money'. Figuring he must have seen me borrowing money off my dad I thanked him and shook his hand.

'Il get the next ones' I said.

He jumped up off his barstool and said 'no ya won't! stop being such a tart and go and join ya mates' he shouted pointing over to Iain doing something strange with a coke can.

I walked over to Iain and patted him on the back 'what's happening here like?'

Iain explained how he can make an empty can of coke move with the power of his mind.

'Bollocks!' I shouted but Colin looked at me as serious as I've ever seen him and said 'it's true I've seen it with my own eyes it's like some sort of gift'.

'Haway you have to show me this Iain' I said sitting in the chair opposite him.

'Very well but my powers may struggle with such skepticism'
Iain said.
He then picked up the empty coke can and poured the remaining few drops from the can onto the table and sat the coke can upright on the puddle of Coca-Cola.
He began rubbing his forehead and started chanting quietly
'Is this the same powers blue summoned when he made the barmaids tits move?' I asked.
'Look non believer' ian shouted nodding towards the can.
I looked at the coke can and noticed surprisingly it was actually turning!.
I looked under the table to see if anything was going on but nothing!. 'How's he doing this?' I said to Colin.
He just looked at me and nodded 'it's a gift'.

The night went on with more dares and laughs in fact I don't think I've ever laughed so much.
'I'm away son the taxi is here are you coming?' my dad slurred being held upright by Dicky.
'I'll just stay a bit longer dad' I said
I was still too busy trying to get the truth out of Iain how he got the coke can to turn I wasn't convinced like Colin was that he had some sort of superhuman powers.
He finally gave in and said 'go and get us a double aftershock and i'll teach you my powers'.
I stumbled my way to the bar bumping into Whoppa nappa on the way making him spill his drink a little down his jumper.
He turned and squared up to me but I just backed away from him held my hands up and apologized and headed to the bar.
A few minutes later I returned to the table with the doubles Iain said 'cheers' and we sank the two red aftershocks and slammed them on the table.
'Right sit there' Iain guided me to the seat where he'd sat  he poured a little drop of a pint of lager  onto the table and plonked the coke can down.
'Right focus! Imagine the coke can turning' he said
'Ok' and I stared for a few seconds and suddenly the can began turning really slowly.
'Bloody hell I'm doing it' I shouted 'how is this possible?' Iain eventually looked up to the ceiling and pointed to the fan above the table. It turned out the combination of the ceiling fan and the liquid on the table makes the can turn. I swore my secrecy to the Iain and the magic circle and carried on drinking raising a glass to Iain's trick.
The rest of the night became a bit of a blur and at some point I left in a taxi a bit worse for the wear.
I woke up in the back of a taxi with a jump and very little recollection of how I got there.
'That'll be four pound fifty' the driver told me.
I rooted about in my pocket and eventually found five pound coins and handed them to the driver 'keep the change' I said as I tried to crawl out the taxi.
I got out the taxi but couldn't get my legs to work properly and I fell to the ground.
The driver got out and helped me to my feet and I thanked him and stumbled towards our house in the square.
I noticed I was uncontrollably veering over to the left so I decided to make a run for it.
I gained a little more speed than I'd planned and I smashed into Harry's wooden fence and privet bushes and fell head first into his neatly kept rose bush sending rose petals and leaves

everywhere.

I let out a scream as the thorns scratched at my face as my head got wedged solid in the base of the rose bush.

The following morning I woke up with the sun shining through my bedroom window stinging my eyes I also had a raging thirst and a pounding headache.

I sat up and realized the pillow was stuck to my face. I peeled off the pillow and noticed my pillow covered in splashes of blood.

I put my hands on my face trying to find where the blood had come from and found three or four little thorns sticking out of my face. I tried to remember what happened to me last night but I couldn't piece it together I could only remember little bits.

I checked my alarm clock it said 8:10.

I jumped out of bed screaming 'dad we've slept in!'.

Noticing luckily I still had my work clothes on so I just quickly sprayed some lynx under my armpits and ran to the bathroom.

I splashed some cold water on my face and glanced in the mirror there was dried blood everywhere and about ten different scratches on my face and neck.

I washed the blood off and pulled a thorn out of my forehead and headed to the landing and banged on my Mam and dads bedroom door.

My dad came to the bedroom door and shouted 'its Saturday man ya tit! and you better go over to Harry's and apologize and fix his fence ya bloody idiot!'.

I wasn't sure what he was on about so I headed back into my room and pulled back the curtains to see the carnage below.

Harry's beloved normally immaculate kept garden was completely ruined! his little wooden picket fence was smashed in pieces and the middle of his privet hedging bush now had a big gaping hole in the middle and his rose bush was completely ruined.

It all came flooding back the dares in the pub, putting a request in on the karaoke for whoppa napper to sing a talking heads song! The fall, the rose bush and I remembered vaguely my Mam dragging me to the toilet after finding me pissing in the kitchen.

I climbed back into bed and covered my sore head with my quilt cover and tried to put my final day at Wear Dockyard behind me.

Chapter seven
A Fresh start.


I got out of bed full of the joys of spring knowing I was starting at the Hepburn yard thinking 'no more John making my life a misery' at least I hoped that was the case. I was sure he would be staying at Wear Dock.

'Your bloody calamities are getting worse!
Please be careful no more falling through roofs' my Mam screamed as I headed out the door.
My Dad was sat behind the wheel impatiently glaring at me as I ran out the door.
I quickly jumped in the passenger seat.
Just as my dad was about to pull away Harry my neighbor came running over to the car I'd purposely avoided him since crashing through his fence that drunken night.
'Where you's off to like Billy? I thought you got paid off' Harry asked
'I got a start at Hepburn with the boy' my dad replied trying to rush his answer as we were running late.
Harry looked at me 'look son I'm going to need a hand tonight to fit Mrs Patterson's bathroom' he said pointing over to our elderly neighbor's house! 'seems as though you wrecked my garden last week it's the least you can do!'
'Aye no bother! I'm really sorry by the way' I groveled as my dad started driving away.

'Bloody hell man! I was supposed to be playing five a side tonight with Pikey and them!' I moaned as we drove off.
'You should learn to handle your bloody drink' My dad shouted while raking about in the side door for his Johnny cash cassette but was getting pissed off as he couldn't find it.
'Your one to talk! that taxi driver thought you were disabled Friday night my Mam told me! He was asking how long you've been like that? and what happened to you?' My Dad just shook his head.

'I've got my charts tape here' I offered as my Dad pulled into the bus stop to pick up Dicky.
'I'm not listening to your shite!' He screamed as Dicky climbed in the back seat.

'Morning lads!' Dicky shouted
'Morning Dicky!' I replied my dad was still too busy raking about for his tape to acknowledge Dicky 'where's that bloody tape?' He shouted leaning over me hunting in the glove box.
'Had four numbers on the lottery on Saturday!'
Dicky shouted 'guess how much?'
'Hundred Quid?' My dad replied.
'I wish! Twenty eight bloody quid! Only two more numbers and I would have won ten million!'
'Disgrace that' my dad shouted.
'Nice villa in Benidorm!'
My dad muttered.
'Eh! What ya on about?' I asked

'The lottery man! If I won the lottery that's what I'd buy!' My dad screamed 'where's that bastard tape!' My dad shouted finally giving up and putting radio two on.
Dicky piped up 'you know what I'd do if I scooped ten million?'
'What's that Dicky' I asked.
'I'd give the wife a million pound and I'd tell her if I ever see her again i'll take it off her!'.

As we whizzed down the A19 my dads fan belt was screeching
'It doesn't sound right that dad! have you heard the noise it's making?'
My dad turned the radio up full blast 'there ya go problem solved!'
Dicky reached over and pointed to the temperature gage that was showing the engine was red hot.
'It'll be reet man' my dad shouted as we headed past the Tyne tunnel with chumbawamba tubthumping blaring out the speakers.
We headed towards Jarrow city centre and I noticed smoke coming out the Bonnet.
'Dad were gonna have to pull over it's gonna catch fire man!'.
'Your a right fanny you man! it's only a bit of smoke!' my dad moaned but eventually gave in and pulled into a shell garage as Dicky also joined in nagging him to stop.

There was a sign up next to the air and water saying out of order so
he pulled up next to a petrol pump.
'You in the AA fawlty?' Dicky asked.
'It's him that can't handle his drink not me!' My dad replied nodding towards me.
'Shall I go buy some water?' I asked my Dad,
But Dicky handed forward a two litre bottle of strawberry flavored fizzy water.
'There ya go fawlty use that'
I jumped out and headed into the garage shop to see if I could buy a bottle of water .

'Get that car away from the pump!!' The Garage bloke screamed over the tannoy. My Dad just ignored him and got out the car and popped the bonnet. The smoke was now hurling out of the engine as my dad began pouring Dicky's strawberry fizzy water in the the cooling tank.

I stood in line waiting to be served with my two litre of Volvic and a red marker pen that was in the bargain bucket for 50p I kept meaning to buy one for marking pipes at work.
The bloke behind the counter screamed over a Mike 'please move your car away from the petrol pump immediately! 'My face was burning red with embarrassment as a few people started slagging my dad off while waiting in line to be served behind me.

I noticed out of the window my Dad drop his bonnet and give the bloke behind the counter the finger.
'Haway man ya tit!' He screamed out the window and sounding his horn to me as I was about to be served.

I threw £1.50 on the counter apologizing and ran out without my change.
I quickly jumped in the car I'd barely got in the passenger seat as my dad sped off shouting

"tosser" to the pissed off bloke behind the counter.

'Hey that smells nice that Dicky' my dad laughed as the smell from the water mixed with smoke came through the vents.

We pulled up at the security gate with smoke hurling out the bonnet the guard pointed us towards the car park with a look of 'what the fuck?' on his face.
We jumped out the car with relief somehow making it although we were half an hour late.
'It'll be alright man just needs to cool down a bit that's all!' my Dad said looking at Dicky and me staring at the smoke billowing from the car.

We finally got into the yard after the journey from hell and the security guard drew us a little map where to find the induction Centre.
We followed the map down the big long bank towards the river Tyne there was a massive green ship sitting in the quay to our right and to our left we could see a massive dry dock which was about three times the size of Wear Dock and sitting in it was an old style white cruise ship.
'That's the Edinburgh castle that there!' Dicky pointed out 'I worked on it years ago but there making it into a Hospital boat now'.
'Some size like' my dad looked on.
We followed the map which lead us to a set of stone steps that took us down to loads of cabins and old workshops.
Then my life took a turn for the worse as I looked over to the building painted green and John Jenkins was stood talking to whoppa napper.
'Late again' John looked at us shaking his head.
'Aye we had a bit of bother on the road like' My Dad replied.
'Where's the induction Centre like John?' Dicky asked.
John pointed over to a little portable office
'Just as well for you lot the safety induction isn't till nine o clock! he said and walked off with whoppa knappa towards the office both of them looking at me like a piece of shit.

We opened the door to the little pokey office and there was a load of familiar faces squeezed into the room that cheered me up straight away.
Colin, Dan, Blue, Decka, Billy Animal, fat kev, Dot and Iain were all there along with a few others and they all cheered as we walked in 'you brought the evening Echo in fawlty?' Blue shouted as we sat down in the only available seats at the front next to Larry who was sat on his own right next to the overhead projector. The projector looked onto a big white screen which had a big photograph of the yard and in big letters it said "welcome to Tyne Tees Dockyard".

I looked back at Iain 'you seen J.J yet?' He frowned and looked at me
'Aye the tosser!'.
Shortly after the room fell silent as a ginger haired bloke walked through the door.
'Alright lads I'm Lenny Douglas I'm going to do your safety induction, it was supposed to be nine o'clock but it looks like it's going to be this afternoon now as I have to attend an important meeting this morning sorry lads!'.

'What we supposed to do till then like?' Billy Animal shouted.

He explained how we could all go sit in the canteen where there's tea and coffee facilities and explained how he needed two apprentices to take the van to Wear Dock to pick up some tools and stuff.

Iain put his hand up and tapped me on the shoulder so I raised my hand too.

'Can one of you drive?' Lenny asked

'Aye, I can!' Iain shouted which was news to me.

Lenny threw ian the keys to Iain and said 'haway lads il show you the van'.

He led us out the side door and pointed to a big white Transit van parked up the road.

'Cheers lads' he said 'there's a few tool boxes to pick up they should be sitting outside the plumbers ready to go' he said and walked away leaving me and Iain with the keys.

'I didn't know you could drive?' I looked at Iain suspiciously

'Why aye I drive my dads car all the time!'.

'Have you passed your test?' I asked.

'Not yet but they don't know that!' he winked.

We opened the big double doors at the back of the van and chucked our rucksacks in then shut the doors and climbed in the front seat and headed up the bank.

Iain pressed a button and there was a locking sound and he sat smiling.

'What?' I asked wondering why he was smiling then suddenly it hit me! The smell of the most horrendous fart I'd ever smelt!

'I began reaching trying to wind down the window to get rid of the smell but it was locked shut.

Iain started laughing his head off and leaned over letting out another loud fart.

He pulled out a AA road map that was on the dashboard and began wafting the smell towards me.

Luckily he had to open his window to ask the security to lift the gate. The young security guard popped his head in the window.

'Dear me who died in there!' He shouted covering his nose.

'Him!' I said Pointing to Iain while nipping my nostrils with my other hand.

We headed down towards the A19 with the smell still lingering in the air.

'What you been eating?'

I asked.

'I was out on the lash all day yesterday stopped off for a curry my guts are rotten!' Iain said holding his stomach.

'You got any pop? I'm choking for a drink!' Iain asked as we sped down the dual carriageway.

'I've got a bottle of water in the back if you pull over i'll get it!' I replied thinking I might get the opportunity to get some fresh air.

Iain eventually pulled over to the hard shoulder of the A19 overlooking Nissan factory. I jumped out taking my chance to take in the fresh air.

I tried to open the back doors to the van but it was locked. Iain tried pressing different buttons but it didn't work so he eventually got out with the keys and tried it in the lock and one of the doors popped open.

My rucksack had slid to the back of the van with Iain's dodgy driving so I climbed up onto the van to get it.

Suddenly I tripped an a metal hook sticking out of the wooden floor and I went flying forward crashing to the floor I got a really sharp pain in my index finger and shrieked in pain as Iain stood laughing holding the door open.
'Shit shit!!' I shouted in horror looking at my finger!.
'What's happened?' Iain shouted jumping in the van running to my aid.
I showed him my finger and he winced in shock as a splinter about two inches long had somehow managed to go right under my nail with blood trickling out.
'It's bloody killing!' I screamed as I looked at it in horror how deep the splinter went!.
'Shit its gone right past the nail' Iain squirmed turning away.
'Shall I pull it out?' I shrieked.
Iain suddenly grabbed my hand turned away from me and quickly pulled the splinter out as I screamed top of my voice with pain.
'There ya gan sorted! Now where's that water?' He said rummaging through my rucksack.
He loosened the top and took a massive swig and said 'ahhhh liquid gold!' Suddenly a gust of wind slammed the van door shut and we were in darkness.

I got myself back to my feet my hand still throbbing but easing a bit since Iain's Doctoring.
Iain was fumbling with the door then looked at me and shook his head.
'What's up?'
I asked barely able to see him in the darkness.
'I think we're locked in' Iain said feeling around the door for some sort of leaver.
'There must be a way to open it from inside surely' I said.
'I can't find it and don't call me Shirley!' He laughed.
'There probably is but it's been boarded out it's all screwed down!' Iain said as I joined in trying to feel round for for a way out.
'Where's the keys?' I asked.
'In the door!' He replied.
'Shit we're screwed! Have you got your phone?. I asked,
'Aye its in the front!' He said and suddenly burst out laughing.

After about ten minutes I was starting to feel very claustrophobic especially with the smell of Iain's constant farting.
I started banging on the side of the van shouting help at the top of my voice.
'We're on a dual carriageway man who's gonna hear ya?' Iain shouted.
'Calm down here's a fag!' he said handing me the cigarette.
'You got a light?' I asked.
'Aye in the front' he said and burst out laughing again.

After another twenty minutes or so I noticed Iain had gone very quiet.

'You ok mate?' I asked.
'No I need a shit!' He said sending me into a blind panic. I felt round every square inch of the van again but all I could find was a paint brush and an empty plastic bucket.

Suddenly Iain broke the silence with a fart and a laugh.
'Haway man if it isn't bad enough!' I shouted covering my nose.

Twenty minutes later we were still stuck in the van with no way out and Iain complaining how he's growing a tail and he's touching cloth.
'Please mate hang on!' I pleaded
'I can't for much longer I'm gonna have to use that bucket!' I could tell by his voice he was deadly serious.
Again I felt around to try find a leaver but nothing! I started kicking the door but all I heard was the keys fall to the ground outside almost teasing me.

'Ten minutes later I heard the unthinkable Iain fumbling around with his belt then a zip 'sorry mate!' He said.

I sat in the opposite corner of the van reaching to be sick as I heard the farts and thuds as his shit hit the bucket.
I had my t shirt shoved up my nostrils to try stop the horrendous smell and I had my fingers in my ears trying to blank out the noise.

Suddenly I was hit in the head with a paintbrush.
'Ow! what was that for?' I asked rubbing my sore head.
'I was trying to get your attention man? have you got a paper in your bag?'
'No why? it's too dark to read anyway' I said not thinking.
'I want to wipe my arse man! I don't wanna read dear deidre!' He snapped back.

'I'm gonna have to use my socks!' he said giving in.

Eventually when Iain finished I think my nose forgot about the putrid smell and we began chatting.
'I can't believe that prick John has been transferred gutted! and Whoppa Napper!' I moaned as Iain started laughing 'he was gonna kill you when you put that song request in the karaoke if it wasn't for Decka he would have' he laughed 'talking heads classic that Reg'.
'Who's Reg?' I asked but Iain shushed me 'listen!' He said 'a car has just pulled up!'.
'Help!!!' I screamed banging on the door then I heard a muffled voice and a cackle over a walkie talkie.
'It's the coppers!' I said to Iain.
'Shit!' Iain muttered.
'Is there somebody in there?' shouted a voice with Authority.
'Aye were locked in' I shouted back.
I heard a rustling of keys then the key going into the lock and suddenly the door opened blinding

me with the light.

A young female police officer with blonde hair tied back popped her head in the van and immediately covered her mouth and nose 'Jesus wept!' She shouted and disappeared out of view. Then a second policeman a bloke in his fifties popped open the other door and looked in and said 'what's going on here?' Covered his mouth and stepped back.
I spotted the female officer over his shoulder throwing up on the grass.

The police were surprisingly lenient quickly hurrying us along after we explained what had happened
I'm not sure if it was the embarrassment or the smell or the fact we were parked on the hard shoulder but they just quickly hurried us on our way to Iain's relief seems as though he only had a provisional license.

We finally arrived at Wear Dockyard and quickly loaded the van with the heavy toolboxes. Although the bucket had gone in the bushes of the A19 the smell was still lingering. 'It's the last time I have a jalfrezi from that place!' Iain laughed as we loaded the last of the boxes into the van.
'Fancy a McDonald's?' Iain asked.
'I'm never eating again after smelling your arse!' I shouted back.

About an hour or so later we ended up back at the Hepburn yard just in time for the induction. We handed Lenny the keys
'Bloody hell it would have been quicker to get the bus!' Lenny laughed as we walked in and took a seat in the induction room.
John looked over shaking his head to Lenny
'Can't be trusted with nothing those two thick as shit!'.
'Right lads were gonna get started in a minute so if anyone needs the bog go now! They are just in the building opposite!' Lenny pointed out.
I jumped out and headed over to the bogs while John looked on shaking his head 'bet he gets lost!'.

I entered the big blue toilet block and was surprised it was a lot cleaner than Wear Dock and actually had soap and paper towels unlike Wear Dock where such luxuries were rare.
I entered the first cubicle which was covered in Graffiti mainly taunts between mackems and Geordies about football but I kept seeing writing slagging John off like 'Mickey mouse wears a J.J watch!' and 'JJ is a baldy prick!' And a big picture drawn of him with a cock on his head.
At least I'm not the only one who hates him I thought and took a bit of comfort knowing he's hated here as much as Wear Dock.
There was also loads of writing about a so called Krusty 'Krusty was here!' also loads of pictures of Krusty the clown from the Simpsons.

I could have sat there all day reading all the graffiti I decided to add my own bit with my newly purchased red pen and wrote 'whoopa nappa's head has 3 orbiting moons!' And drew a picture of the prick on the toilet door.

I eventually headed back to the induction room where nobody said a word as they were too busy laughing at Billy Animal who was taking the piss out of fat kev because of how tight he is with money.
'He's so tight he turns the gas off when he flips his bacon man!' He shouted as the room erupted into laughter.
Lennie was banging on about safety but could hardly be heard over the laughing and carrying on.
Lennie didn't seem too bothered but John's face going increasingly red then he suddenly stood up and yelled 'haway man for fuck sake shut up! give Lennie some respect you bunch of children!'
'What's it to you ya baldy prick your not the Gaffa here!' Decka shouted over and John sat down quietly two seats along from us.
Me and Iain we were both smirking hearing the news for the first time that John was working on the tools.

The room fell silent after the outburst and Lennie carried on talking about working at heights and harnesses.

Shortly after he moved onto smoking 'right lads from April there stopping smoking on all  Ships as the company is having a bit of a no smoking campaign so any ideas you have about helping people stop it would be a good help, were going to be giving away free nicotine patches that sort of stuff so if anyone is interested see me!'.
Blue raised his hand 'Women are like cigarettes!'
'How?' Lennie asked looking confused wondering what the hell he was talking about.
'Well they cost a fortune!, ones never enough, they'll bloody kill you in the end!,
He laughed
'And they make your fingers stink!'
Billy Animal chipped in,
'and you wanna set fire to them!' John shouted.
'No that's just you John because your a horrible bullying twat!' Decka shouted which set the whole room off laughing.

After an hour or so of boring videos and form filling in we were allowed to start work and meet our new bosses.
We were pointed in the direction of the plumbers shop which was over the other side of the Dock so the eight of us pipe fitters headed over there while the others went to there places of work.

When we got to the plumbers shop we walked in the big main door and it was huge compared to the little workshop in Wear Dock.
There was about ten work benches with blokes stood round chatting there was also loads of machine saws and drills and benders and it was spotless compared to the our old shop, all the

pipes were stacked up neatly on racks in order of size and there was even a overhead crane which one of the lads was using to lift a pipe out the rack.
'This is more like it!' Said Decka as we headed into the office in the middle of the workshop.

'Alright lads here come the mackems!, 'proper pipefitters' a little grey haired bloke stood up to greet us shaking our hands asking our names.
He got to my Dad and said 'I don't need your name fawlty!' and started laughing shaking his hand 'I worked with you in Thompson's years ago!,
Jimmy whistler remember me?'
'Why aye! alright mate how's it going!' My dad laughed.
'This is my son Andrew!' He said patting me on the shoulder!' I shook his hand and he told me how he once met me when I was about 3 years old.

After we had made our introductions to Jimmy our new boss he told us to just hang around the workshop for the day and make ourselves at home and meet the other lads.
My Dad,Dot and Dicky knew quite a few of the lads from the shipyards in Sunderland from back in the seventies and eighties and seemed to have a little story attached to each person like big Brian who in is day was more accident prone than me my dad said 'hey remember that time you were up dancing in steels club!' he said both of them in stitches of laughter.
Big Brian told us he was once dancing swinging his legs about that much that he got his foot caught in a blokes pocket! unlucky for the bloke at the time he was carrying a full tray of drinks.

Brian was a tall thin bloke in his early fifties and was a dead ringer for Russ Abbott an eighties comedian.
'Take notice of this bloke here lads!' He's the best in the business he's forgotten more than I've ever known!' My dad said to me and Iain with his arm round Brian's shoulder.

Just as everyone was laughing and joking around I noticed whoppa napper walking towards us with a light switch in one hand with wires popping out the bottom 'alright lads has any of you lads got a red marker pen by any chance?' he said looking over at me, Iain and Decka stood chatting.
'Aye I've got one you can borrow!' I said rooting round in my pocket for my pen.
'So it's you who's been writing on the bog wall about me you little Bastard!' he shouted lunging forward to grab me but I was too quick and I scarpered out the door leaving everyone laughing their heads off behind me.

About half an hour later I peeped my head in the plumbers shop and whoppa napper had finally gone I casually strolled back in and joined in with my dad talking to someone with his back to me.
'This is the boy Andrew!' my Dad said to the ginger Curly haired bloke he turned to look at me and I couldn't help but laugh he was the spitting double of krusty the clown from the Simpsons.
He looked at me wondering what I was laughing at I apologised and shook his hand.
My dad gave me a strange look and said 'this is K... Dave Thirlwell!'
Hearing my Dad almost calling him krusty set me off laughing again.

'Sorry I just can't stop laughing at a joke I heard earlier!'
He just looked at me a little confused and smiled then I heard one of the lads do an amazing krusty the clown laugh and it sent me off in a hysterical laughing fit so I ran out the shop again and when I got outside bent over and laughed my head off.

Iain came out a few minutes later to see what was going on.
I explained the krusty crack which set him off laughing.

Iain handed me a fag and we sat outside in the sun enjoying our fags in the sunshine.
'Bit of a result this Reg!'
Iain said
'Aye I think I'm taking to this place like'
I agreed.

As we stood there smoking fat kev came over with a big stocky bloke with dark hair in his early twenties he wandered up with his safety helmet clutched under his arm 'alright lads im Mick' he said reaching out shaking our hands as we introduced ourselves.
Fat kev asked Iain if he could pinch a fag Iain got his pack out and handed him one and a lighter.
We stood chatting about the place how it was much better than Wear Dock then Mick announced he was going to speak to Someone and headed inside.
'Full of shit him by the way don't believe a word that comes out his mouth!' Kev said nodding towards Mick.
'He seems areet!' Iain replied.
'He is! he's sound as a pound but he constantly lies it's like he can't help himself!, if I've been to Tenerife he's been to elevenarife you know what I mean' kev said chuckling away to himself.
'He's called Mick Fleetwood but the lads call him Fleetwood mac' he said stubbing his fag out' he told us all once he was going to Miami for his holidays and one of the lads seen him in Magaluf' he laughed then headed in the shop singing 'tell me lies tell me sweet little lies!'.
I was just about to head in my self but I was suddenly grabbed from behind and put in a headlock.
'You gonna stop calling me whoppa napper you little prick' he yelled as he squeezed my neck tighter as Iain looked on laughing.
'Aye sorry!' I squealed as his grip got tighter.
He swung me round which sent me flying into the bins that was sat next to the door. I climbed up the door to get to my feet and he punched me in the ribs.
'Alright that's enough you prick!' Iain shouted and pulled Whoppa nappa back.
'This isn't over!' He yelled in my face and stormed off into the plumbers shop.
'Bloody hell that was a bit harsh!' Iain said helping me to my feet.
'I was only having a laugh with the prick!' I replied 'I thought he was only messing about at first but the Dickhead was serious!'.

An hour or so after the carry on with Whoppa nappa I decided to leave it and hope things would blow over and I thought I'd just keep out of his way.

I stood chatting to my Dad about the car

'Tommy one of the lads is fixing my car for me in the fitters shed so you don't have to worry apparently it's only a bracket come loose which is why the fan belt is ...'

My dad waffled on but I wasn't really listening I was too busy wondering what to do about Whoppa nappa.

I didn't want to go running to Decka again but I wasn't going to put up with his bullying I thought.

'Anybody in there?' My dad shouted waving a hand in front of my face.

'Sorry Dad I was miles away' I said.

'You ok son?' He asked suddenly all serious.

'Aye champion' I replied and wandered off to the toilets.


I sat there on the toilet pondering what to do when i heard someone go in the next cubicle.

I sat reading the graffiti 'fleetwood Mack choked Linda lovelace'

It made me laugh after hearing kev saying he was always talking shit.

Suddenly out of nowhere I heard a noise above me and I looked up and a massive bucket of swarfega soap was emptied over me.

I quickly pulled up my pants and jeans and threw on my overalls and opened the toilet door and seen whoppa napper there creased with laughter when he seen me covered in the bright green sticky soap.

I looked in the mirror I looked like I'd just been gunked on noels house party.

Even I found it funny when I saw myself in the mirror.

I looked at him

Pondering my next move.

I put my green swarfega covered hand out in front of me and said

'Look we have got off to a bad start I'm sorry for the drawing it was just a joke and I didn't know you didn't like being called that! So it's up to you we sort this outside or shake on it here and now and forget the whole thing!'

I was thinking to myself 'shit If he chooses to take me outside he will kill me! I'm good at hurting myself not other people!'

He stared into my eyes and said 'look..'

Just then Dickie walked in and started laughing at me 'bloody hell Andy what's happened?'

I smirked and said 'some twat got me with swarfega when I was on the bog!'

Whoppa nappa walked out as I explained to Dicky I sat there having a dump and someone chucked the bucket over me.

I got myself cleaned up best I could with the paper towels but my arse was itching like mad as the swarfega even got in my boxer shorts.


I headed back in the workshop eventually after cleaning myself up. My dad was stood there dressed ready to leave 'haway man ya tit hurry up it's time to go man!'

I quickly got my overalls off again chucked them in the corner of the workshop and followed him up the bank.


Back in the car my dad was just about to jump in the driver seat when he seen a cassette sat in the driver seat.

'I must have been sat on the bastard' he shouted and popped it in the cassette player and ring of fire came blasting out the speakers.

We eventually arrived back home in our square and outside of Mrs Patterson's house was a big yellow skip with an old green toilet, sink and a big pile of broken tiles and concrete.
'Shit I forgot about helping Harry!' I moaned. My Dad headed in the house and I headed towards Mrs Patterson's house next door.
I knocked on the little brass knocker on the old wooden door but got no answer so I popped my head in the window and seen Mrs Patterson jump to her feet she was waving to me and made her way to the front door.
Eventually after hearing her rattling about with keys the door opened and she let me in.
Mrs Patterson must have been about 90 nobody knew how old as she always said none of your business when anyone asked she also never told anyone her first name.
She was in good shape though for her age however old it was,she walked to the shops no problem but her face was so old full of wrinkles.
She was a lovely old soul who took a shine to me but seemed to hate everyone else.
She told me Harry was upstairs so I headed up and she gave my bum a squeeze as I moved past her.
'Hey I'm not that old you know!' and she gave me a wink and a smile.
I quickly scarpered upstairs to the bathroom and seen the crack of Harry's arse as he was bent over the toilet fastening it to the wall.
'Hey you've done a canny job Harry!' I said as I admired the pretty impressive bathroom all gold taps and brilliant white ceramic bathroom suite.
'I'm just about done now! It's took me all day!' He said 'what can I do to help?' I asked wondering what use I could be to him.
'Il just need a lift with her old bath! Weighs a bloody ton!, actually you can see if you can get that flusher working! She insisted on an old style pulley chain! It was a pain in the arse to fit but I can't get it to flush!' He said taking off his glasses and cleaning them on his t shirt.
'Is it ok to stand on this?' I said pointing to the toilet.
'Aye just be careful it's took me all day to get this far'
I carefully climbed onto the toilet bowl and reached up to to the old style flushing cistern fastened about a six foot off the ground.
I very carefully removed the ceramic lid handing it down to Harry.
I looked Inside and pulled the chain.
I noticed the ballcock was catching against the side of the systen so I gently tried to bend the rod attached to the ball cock to try and free it getting caught on the Cistern.
I explained to Harry what the problem was and he passed me up a pair of big heavy Stilson grips.
I gently gripped the bar and twisted it freeing the ballcock from the side of the Cistern 'try that Harry!' He pulled the chain and to my amazement it worked 'wow your a natural son!' He smiled and handed me the ceramic lid.
Still having the stilsons in my hand it was a bit tricky to put back on but I was very careful and I just about managed it. I carefully lay the stilsons on top of the Cistern and tried the chain again 'result!' Shouted Harry as he helped me down from the toilet bowl.

'Right now the bathtub!' Harry said pointing to the bedroom to my left.

'It's cast iron so be careful' he said grabbing the tap end I struggled with the weight of the other end but managed to lift it and maneuvered it to the stairs I headed down first as Harry clung onto the top easing it down the stairs.

We somehow managed to lift it down the stairs and after a few minutes of struggle we got it out of the front door into the skip.

'Right Mrs Patterson were all done! Wanna see?' said Harry 'I've just got to have a quick clean up and get my tools and we'll leave you in peace!' Harry said wiping sweat from his brow.

'It's always nice to have young men round the place she smiled and winked at me!'

Then she tried to give a big wad of ten pound notes to Harry who point blank refused 'No,no no!, please put your money away or i'll never help you again' Harry shouted looking very insulted 'quick hurry up before she asks again' Harry said pushing me up the stairs.

We went back into the bathroom and Harry began putting his tools away while I bent over with the dustpan and brush picking up the bits of dust.

Mrs Patterson walked in and seen me bent over and said 'ooooo very nice!' Harry laughed as we stood up ready to go.

'Wow very posh I love it thanks Harry' she said admiring his very professional job.

Just as we were about to leave I noticed the stilsons still sat on top of the cistern.

I told Harry he said 'grab them for me will you?' So I stepped onto the side of the toilet bowl and reached up for the stilsons, just as I touched the handle my foot slipped off the side of the toilet and went into the toilet itself and then I fell backwards to the floor with a crash with my foot still stuck in the toilet, then I looked up seen the stilsons wobble on the top of the Cistern, suddenly they tipped off the edge and came crashing down smashed against the side of the sink breaking a big chunk off the side of the sink then crashed onto the toilet bowl which cracked the bowl then the whole thing broke completely in half releasing my foot and covering the bathroom floor with water.

I lay on the floor in shock and looked over to Harry and Mrs Pattison stood open mouthed.

'Oh Dear!' said Mrs Patterson as I stumbled to my feet.

Harry looked at me like he was going to kill me when I handed him the stilsons.

'Sorry!' I shouted and legged it down the stairs and out of the door as quickly as I could.

Remembering the cricket bat incident I thought I'd better go to Pikey's to hide out rather than go home.

Chapter 8
The thief.

'We've slept in again!' My dad yelled that quickly snapped me out of my wonderful sleep.
All my worries came flooding back, Harry,Whoppa napper! I was wondering which one was going to kill me first.
My Dad popped his head in my room again 'haway man get up ya tit!'.
I quickly got out of bed and got my work clothes on, sprayed some lynx under my pits and ran down the stairs where my Mam gave me my rucksack and popped a piece of toast in my mouth and I quickly ran outside and jumped in the passenger seat of my Dads car.
Luckily there was no sign of Harry but the skip was still there with the broken sink and toilet sitting on the top of the pile of rubble.
My dad quickly sped out the square and I breathed a sigh of relief as we drove up St Luke's road.
'You owe me a hundred Quid!'
my dad yelled
'What?' I gasped.
'You heard me Harry was raging last night when you scarpered! I had to drive down to B and Q with him to calm him down and buy a new bog and sink! And bloody fit it!' My dad moaned.
'Shit I'm sorry Dad!' I looked on shocked.
'You would have been sorry if Harry got hold of you last night! Where did you go anyway I never heard you come in?'
I stayed round Pikey's after footy for a bit his Mam made me some tea!'
I replied gutted wondering how I was gonna pay the hundred quid back.
'Right straight after work get your arse to the shops get Harry some cans and Mrs Patterson some chocolates and go and apologise!' My Dad ordered.
I agreed 'can I borrow £20?' I asked.

We arrived at the bus stop and Dicky jumped in 'morning lads' he shouted.
'Morning Dicky!' Me and dad shouted back at the same time.
'Remember you said you'd pick fat Kev up fawlty!' Dicky reminded my Dad 'shit I forgot all about that!' My dad snapped looking at his watch.
We headed down South Hylton bank and Dicky spotted fat Kev stood at the bus stop 'there he is Basil!' Dicky pointed over.

'Morning lads!' Kev shouted as he got in the back stinking of drink.
'Thought i might have missed you! I slept in went out for a few last night' Kev shouted forward to my dad.
'Bloody hell you smell like Duncan disorderly!' My dad replied.
'Hey fawlty would you mind stopping off for fleetwood mac on the way past Hastings hill? He was in the club last night and I said I'd ask you' kev asked my dad who didn't look very happy but agreed anyway.
'What's up like is his Ferrari getting fixed like?' Dicky laughed.
'He's full of shit man he told the lads he cycles all the way to work in thirty minutes, Billy Animal

seen him getting off the train with his bike yesterday morning!, anyway he's bikes knackered he left it at work so that's why he's asked for a lift!' Kev said shaking his head.

'Where is he?' My dad shouted pulling into the Hastings hill pub car park and there was no sign of him.

We sat there for a few minutes still no sign of him so my Dad suggested we go to his house.
'Do you know where he lives kev?' My dad asked looking in his rear view mirror at him.
'Aye Krusty gave us a lift last night we dropped him off at the big posh house at the top of Sevenoaks drive' kev pointed up the road so we headed round there.
'Hey it's a lovely area this like, worth a few bob these pads!' Dicky commented as we pulled up to a big posh house where Kev pointed out fleetwood Mac lived.
We drove up to the immaculate four bedroomed detached house with double gates with two concrete sculptured lions on the top of the pillars.
My dad pulled up in his clapped out Volvo and began sounding the horn 'haway Mick!' He yelled out the car window.
We sat and waited a few minutes as a few curtains twitched but still no sign of Mick.
'Andrew go and give him a knock!' My dad yelled.
So I got out walked up to the house and pushed open the big wooden gates and walked up the drive of the house there was a black brand new sporty looking Mercedes parked on the drive which I admired as a walked past.
I rang the bell on the expensive looking double  glass doors and heard a musical chime.
A couple of minutes later I seen movement behind the glass doors and the doors eventually opened. A little grey haired bloke in his sixties dressed in striped pyjamas and slippers looked at me suspiciously 'yes?' He said in a posh voice.
'Is Michael here? We're here to pick him up for work!' I asked.
'Michael?' He said 'there's nobody lives here called Michael!'.
'Very sorry must be the wrong house! Do you know a Michael Fleetwood?' I asked
'I've lived here for thirty years son and I've never heard that name!' 'Sorry to have bothered you!' I said and ran out to the car.

'He doesn't live there!' I said as I climbed in.
'He's full of shit!' Kev shouted 'he probably lives at Pennywell the lying bastard!'
My Dad sped off back down the road and there was Mick Fleetwood stood outside the Hastings Hill pub.
My Dad pulled up and mick jumped in 'cheers fawlty!' He shouted as he jumped in wondering why we were all staring at him open mouthed.

'Ya full of shit!' Kev shouted.
'What you on about?' Mick shouted back.
We've just been to your house you said you lived in! some old bloke answered the door said he'd never heard of you!' Kev shouted getting annoyed.
'That's my Dad he's got Dementia man!' Mick snapped back.
'I bet that's your Mercedes parked in the drive an all is it?' Kev shouted 'No that's my mams,

they're staying with us for a while' mick replied.
'Aye about thirty year' I whispered to my dad He looked at me confused and put the radio on and Natalie Imbruglia torn came on my Dad turned it up to cover Kev and Mick arguing in the back.
We eventually got to the Dockyard and pulled up in the car park next to the security gate and we all got out and walked down the bank.

When we got to the workshop all the lads were stood there looking at the notice board there was a sign that said "Safety officers wanted No experience needed all training will be given" and underlined it said "permanent position If interested please sign below"
'Il have some of that!' My dad said signing his name below underneath John Jenkins name.
'Put my name down!' Krusty shouted over, my Dad couldn't resist he wrote in big  letters "KRUSTY".
Everyone started laughing apart from Krusty who snatched the pen scribbled Krusty out and wrote "David Thirlwell".

I ran to put my overalls and helmet on before anyone noticed I was late. I found them where I'd left them and climbed into the legs then put my hand in the arms only to find they'd been cut off 'bastards!' I muttered as I kicked off my trainers and went to put my boots on I slipped my foot in the left boot and went to move but the boot was stuck solid to the floor.
Iain seen me struggling and came over laughing 'what's happening?' He asked as I eventually managed to get my foot back out and noticed my boots had been screwed to the floor.
Jimmy seen us and came over 'someone been playing funny buggers young en?' Jimmy asked
'Aye' I replied showing him the boots screwed to the floor.
'Haway lads there's a meeting in the bait room! Afterwards you can go to the store and get some new boots and overalls and a locker so the buggers can't get at them' jimmy said patting me on the back and walking away.
'Seems sound him!' I said to Iain.
'Aye big change from the baldy prick' Iain replied.

Five minutes later we were all gathered in the bait hut for our meeting. It was big enough to hold all 15-20 pipefitters.
The room was quiet and we heard a whistling getting louder and in walked Jimmy whistling followed by two other blokes wearing white overalls.
'Right lads this won't take long!, just want to warn you all there's a thief about! there's tools going missing even food just wanted to ask you to keep your valuables in your lockers or don't bring them to work at all'.
I started suddenly going red for some unknown reason I always do in these situations my brain tells me they're all thinking it's you! Even though it wasn't.
As I sat there burning up Iain looked on suspiciously 'what's up with you?' He whispered
'This always bloody happens! It used to happen at school!' I explained getting redder and redder a few people noticed which made it even worse.
'Anyone caught will be sacked immediately! Personally I can't think of anything worse than stealing off your own work mates, but these things happen! Just be vigilant lads!' Jimmy said

shaking his head.

The taller bloke behind him piped up 'can you return all tools to the store please lads we just want to count up everything see what's missing, and for you lads that don't know me I'm Ronnie by the way and this ugly bastard is Tommy!' he pointed over to the big heavy set bloke with dark hair stood next to him.

'Alright lads the bloke wants his boat' jimmy smiled and walked out whistling.

There was a bit of chatter as the bait room emptied and a few people put sandwiches in the fridge and pies in the oven as they walked out.

Big Brian whispered in my dad's ear and put a big sausage roll in the big glass oven and a big bottle of Pepsi in the fridge.

Me and Iain headed out to the office and jimmy called us in.

The two other bosses were rolling about on the floor fun fighting, Ronnie had Tommy in a head lock and he was rolling round trying to escape as me and Iain looked on laughing.

'Ignore them two nutters here's your keys for your lockers get yourselves over to the store get new overalls and boots here's a chitty!' he said handing us a piece of paper each and our locker keys as the two bosses screamed at each other in the corner.

Just as me and Iain were walking past the Dock towards the store I heard whoppa napper behind me laughing and joking walking about ten meters behind us heading the same way as us.

'Don't look now but I think whoppa napper is walking behind us' I said to Iain who instantly turned round and looked.

'Aye he is Reg!' He replied.

'Why did you turn round man?' I said discreetly.

'He wasn't looking anyway he's with superted!' He laughed.

'Superted?' I said looking puzzled. I couldn't help but look Myself wondering who superted was so I looked round at whoppa napper who was walking and talking to a small stocky lad with glasses on and another lad in his late teens even taller and thinner than me and a face full of acne.

'Which ones superted?' I asked still baffled.

'The little one with glasses' Iain said smirking.

'Why do they call him superted then?' I said thinking he looks nothing like superted!.

'Have you seen his mate?' Iain said laughing.

I still didn't get it and was still thinking about it when we walked in the store.

The store at this Dockyard like everything else was a lot more modern and seemed to have everything, it was huge with a little counter at the front.

Larry came to the counter smiling as always 'alright bonny lads this place is more like it eh? Anyway what can I do you for?' Me and Iain handed him our notes of paper.

'Stick your boot sizes and overall sizes on there Larry said giving us back the bits of paper and a little blue bookies pen.

We were busy filling the forms in when the door opened behind us and Whoppa nappa walked in with Superted and the spotty lad.

It then dawned on me when I seen the spotty lad close up why they call his mate superted and I burst out laughing. Whoppa napper stared at me for a little while and then walked out of view as I carried on filling the form in.

A few Awkward minutes later Larry passed the overalls and boots over and said 'try them on make sure they fit!' Which we did and me and Iain stood there nodding at each other.

'Aye there areet!' Iain said and Larry gave us a yellow helmet each.

'The apprentices here have to wear yellow hats, here you go!' We popped our hats on and signed a form ticking the items we received.

Suddenly Larry looked at me and started laughing.

'What?' I asked 'yellow definitely isn't your colour! Next!' He shouted and whoppa napper went to the counter ignoring me and Iain.

Iain looked at me and laughed 'what?' I said and Iain said the same 'Larry's right yellow isn't your colour' I walked out the store and superted and spotty both looked at me and laughed too 'is it that bad?' I laughed myself. Me and Iain headed out the store.

I couldn't help but feel paranoid with everyone laughing but soon forgot about it as we headed on our way over to the plumbers workshop.

We walked over the Dock gate and I could hear someone shouting in the distance I looked about but couldn't see anyone.

Then again I heard it 'knobhead!' I looked up and Billy animal was on his way up the crane ladder laughing shouting 'knobhead!' I looked at Iain puzzled.

'What's he on about?'

Iain just laughed and said 'god knows he's off his head!'.

My dad was walking towards me laughing with Dickie and Krusty both smirking, none of them had any boots and overalls on and they all had their bags on their shoulders.

'Where you going like?' I asked

'We are going on night shift were off home' my dad replied

'How's I gonna get home?' I asked.

'Don't worry knobhead! I've left my car keys in your bag you can drive home! you've got your provisional haven't you? And Kev will be going with you he can drive if your scared!' My dad said while I looked at him a little shocked after hearing him calling me a knobhead!.

'How you getting home then?' I asked

'Kk... Dave is taking me home' my dad laughed having nearly saying Krusty again.

'You'll have to get in yourself somehow tomorrow though son' my dad said.

As we headed for the plumbers shop Kev came up to us smirking.

'Alright lads! I'm leaving! I've just been fixed up with a nice job in Norway' he said rubbing his hands together.

'Any chance you can bring the car down later so I can chuck my toolbox in the boot, I've put my notice in I'm finishing at the end of the shift' Kev said looking very pleased with himself.

'Aye no bother mate il have a word with Jimmy whistler make sure it's ok'
I replied.

As me and Iain walked in the plumbers shop there was a big cheer and Dot shouted over
'knobhead' I realized there must have been a reason people kept calling me that.
I put my hand on top of my helmet and felt something on the top.
I took my helmet off and there was a six inch cock made out of insulating foam stuck to my to
my hat with double sided duct tape.
'The bastard was that whoppa napper?' I laughed.

Jimmy came whistling over to us 'aright lads put your stuff in your lockers, you're gonna give
Brian a hand on the fresh water'
He said pointing us to the bait room.
We headed in and we soon found our lockers Brian followed us in and he slid the oven door
open and said 'it's still there!'.
Me and Iain put our stuff in our new lockers and looked at Brian examining his sausage roll.
'Some bugger nicked my pie yesterday I know who it was I'm positive, just got to prove it' he
said and winked placing his sausage roll back in the oven.

We headed back out into the workshop and Brian asked how my brother was
'Aye he's champion I didn't know you knew him!' I replied
'Aye he's mates with my eldest' he explained.

Brian explained what job he was doing and talked us through it and drew a little sketch on the
bench with chalk.
 Me and Iain just looked on baffled.
Brian explained how we have a lot to learn but over time we will pick it up and any problems we
could always come to him.

He seemed like a decent bloke I thought while he started showing us how to use the hand
benders.

suddenly there was a big shout came from the canteen Brian suddenly stopped what he was
doing and ran over me and Iain followed.

Fleetwood mick was in there with a pie on the floor.
Brian stared at him and said 'what you up to mick?'
Eying him up suspiciously
'I was just checking my pie see if it's cooked and I've burned the bloody thing I pulled it out but
burned my hand' he said holding his hand blowing on his fingers.
'What did you think I was doing like?, I'm not the bloody thief!' Mick shouted looking a little
pissed off.
'Hey I never said you were!' Brian said heading back out into the workshop.
'My Dad's gone on night shift I've got his car keys though if you need a lift' I said watching Mick

scoop his burned pie off the floor.

'Aye cheers, my bike still isn't fixed'.

I explained I hadn't passed my test but as long as him or kev had a driving license I'd be fine.

We headed out to see Brian for the next hour or so, he taught us how to make offsets in pipes all the while keeping an eye on who was coming and going in the canteen.

'Right lads breaktime!' We went off to wash our hands then followed Brian into the canteen 'there ya go got the bastard!' Brian shouted pointing to a sausage roll on the floor.

A few blokes came over to see what he was on about 'look I pushed a big wooden peg inside the sausage roll and put it in the oven and someone's tried to bite into it!' He said pointing to it on the floor.

'Hey thats half a tooth there look!' One of the lads pointed next to the sausage roll.

'Who's not here?' Brian said looking round the room.

Me and Iain eventually sat down at a table at the back of the room and watched carefully as each person walked in to see if they were missing a tooth.

'Dots not here!, Kevin's not here, Fleetwood mac's not here

Decka isn't here!' Brian shouted just as Decka walked in.

'What's up? Decka asked noticing the room had gone quiet since he'd came in.

Brian explained about the peg and the tooth.

Decka laughed as he examined the tooth 'hey that's a front tooth that! well done Brian lad' he laughed patting him on the back.

A few minutes later JJ walked in and sat down and started reading his paper without a saying a word.

'Aright John?' Decka shouted over to which he looked confused as he looked over his Daily mirror and just nodded.

Me and Iain looked at each other thinking the same thing wondering if it was him.

'You heard anything about the safety officers job yet like?' Brian asked looking at John.

'Na not yet! I only signed the form this morning' he said as the room made a sort of disappointed groan as his teeth seemed in tact.

He looked round wondering what was going on when the door opened and Micky Fleetwood walked in singing 'no...matter what! they tell you....no matter what they do..' he suddenly stopped realizing everyone was looking at him.

'What? It's won awards this voice man!' He shouted and sat down opposite john.

The door opened again and kev walked in picked his bag up off the table and quickly walked back out.

'It's got to be him!' Brian shouted.

'He's a tight Bastard aye but he's not a thief surely' Decka shouted.

'Well where's he gone? Actions of a guilty man that's all I'm saying!' Brian said sitting down picking up his paper.

The door opened and Dan walked in all eyes quickly turned to him as he looked on wondering what was going on, he sat down opposite me and Iain as everyone watched him carefully

'what's going on?' he whispered running his hand over his hat making sure he didn't have a big cock on top like I did earlier.

We explained what had happened and he showed his full set of teeth off to everyone who looked on and they carried on reading there papers.

'You seen fat kev?' I asked 'Aye he's sitting outside in the sun with his top off! what a site' he said laughing.

'Prime suspect!' Iain muttered.

After dinner we headed out into the workshop and jimmy asked us to go back in the bait room for a toolbox talk I went out to tell fat kev but there was no sign of him but his rucksack was still there.

I followed the rest of the lads back in the bait hut and we sat back down in our seats.

'Right lads this won't take long 'were starting an overtime rota' jimmy said pinning a sheet up next to the microwave.

'If any of you want to work Saturday or Sunday put your names on the sheet,

Also we're missing two pairs of stilsons out of the store if anyone has them bring them back please.'

He said and walked out whistling.

We headed back into the workshop and Brian eventually came out and carried on where he left off showing us how to bend offsets in pipes.

We stood there trying to take in everything he was saying when Iain nodded to me I looked round and fat kev was heading into the canteen with his bag.

Brian didn't notice and carried on chatting away.

Dot came over watching Brian and when Brian looked at him he gave him a teething smile.

'I heard I was a suspect like!' Dot shouted 'all the years you've known me!' He said shaking his head.

'I never said you were a suspect!' Brian shouted back.

'Hey you know who ya mates are!' He said wandering off winking at me and Iain.

The afternoon dragged on and eventually jimmy came round giving all the new lads a clock card and pointed to the clocking machine where we had to swipe our cards when we leave.

'No clocking each other out there's a camera up there!' jimmy said pointing to a camera up in the ceiling above the clock.

'Jimmy is it ok to bring my dads car down here? Kev wants to put his tools in the boot as I'm dropping him off tonight' I asked Jimmy

'Aye no bother son, you better go now though as there's not long left'.

I quickly ran in the canteen to my locker to get the car keys out of my bag and ran up the bank as quick as I could.

When I got to the security hut I explained to the young security guard

I needed to drive the car in the yard he passed me a green pass and told me to stick it on the dashboard.

I ran over to the car park and jumped in my dad's car and drove up to the security barrier I stopped with a jump and stalled the car as the guard lifted the barrier to let me through.

I eventually pulled up outside the plumbers shop and seen Kev standing outside with his rucksack and tools. I quickly threw the keys to him and ran inside to get ready to go.

I quickly ran to my locker and took my helmet and overalls off and chucked them in the locker and quickly put my trainers on and ran to join the line for the clocking machine.
I noticed Jimmy at the front of the line looking in everyone's bags as they clocked out.
Kev at the front shook his head zipped his rucksack up and headed to the car.
Fleetwood Mick did the same I eventually got to the end of the line swiped my clock card and opened rucksack for Jimmy to have a look inside.
Jimmy took the rucksack and looked inside.
'Sorry to have to do this son! see you in the morning' he said handing me back my bag back.
I ran to the car outside the plumbers shop Fleetwood mac was sitting in the back seat and Kev was in the front.
'Sorry to keep you waiting lads!' I said as Kev handed me the keys.
I turned the key in the ignition and began reversing but stalled.
Mick laughed
'Take your time' he said and I tried again this time successfully reversing out and shuddered up the bank.
The security guard waved us through and I handed him the green pass and tried to drive through the barrier and stalled again.
I started the car up again and off we went.
'I used to be a driving instructor you know! I'll give you some lessons if you want' mick shouted from the back.
'Bollocks!' Kev shouted as I stalled yet again at a roundabout.
'It's true I used to work for B.S.M.' Mick shouted leaning over from the back seat.

I managed to get the car going again and headed down towards the A19.
'Hey I can't believe they searched us for them stilsons on the way out!' Mick shouted.
'Bit out of order like!' I replied.
'It's a good thing he didn't look in your boot!' Kev said smiling with half his front tooth missing.
'Ya fucking joking ain't ya' shouted Fleetwood Mac.
'Hey there loaded man they'll not miss a couple of pairs of stilsons' Kev shouted back.

Ten minutes or so later I pulled off the A19 to Sunderland and carried on to Pennywell.
'Shit sorry Mick I've drove past yours I'll drop kev off first then turn round!' I said looking in the mirror at Mick.
I pulled in at a bus stop and Kev jumped out I opened the boot and he got his tools and the two pairs of stilsons he nicked as I watched him shaking my head.
'Cheers Andy, probably see you around' kev said and headed down the road loaded up with bags and boxes.
I quickly ran in the shop next to the bus stop and picked up some cans for Harry and a big box of milk tray for Mrs Patterson and jumped back in the car and chucked them on the back seat next to Mick.
A bus was sounding his horn for me to move from the bus stop so I started stressing trying to

get my seatbelt on as quick as I could.

I tried to pull away as quick as I could but I stalled again.

My nerves got the better of me and the bus driver was sounding his horn as I stalled for a second time as I moved into the road and a car had to slam his breaks on to avoid hitting me.

'Jump out mate il drive'

Mick said quickly jumping out the back seat and opening the drivers door.

I quickly got out and jumped in the passenger seat as Mick drove us away from the angry drivers.

'You've just got to take your time man! Don't stress' Mick said as we headed back up South Hylton bank.

'Haway go and drop your stuff off and ask your Dad if I can take you for a lesson, I need to go to boldon anyway pick a crank up for my bike!' Mick said as he turned onto My road.

'Down here isn't it?' He asked.

'Aye first square after the bus terminus!' I replied.


We pulled into the square and I quickly jumped out and ran to Mrs Patterson's house and knocked on her door.

I waited a couple of minutes but there was no sign of her so I popped my head in the window and she seen me and quickly jumped out of her chair waving and came to the door.

After a couple of minutes of hearing sounds of rustling of keys and bolts being unlocked.

The door flew open and Mrs Patterson reached out to give me a hug.

I gave her a Hug and kissed her on the cheek and handed her the chocolates and apologized for the toilet and the sink.

'You didn't have to do that you silly sod!' she said and smiled.

I explained I was in a rush and waved goodbye and she stood waving at the door as I ran to Harry's house.

I opened Harry's gate and rang the bell and a few seconds later the door opened and his little brown boxer dog shot out the door and out the gate.

'Bloody hell man!' Harry shouted chasing after him.

Seeing what had happened Mick jumped out the car door and quickly managed to chase the dog and grab him by his black spiked Collar before he escaped out the square.

Harry ran out relieved getting Rambo back and thanked Mick 'he's a topper I used to breed these' Mick said handing the collar to Harry. Harry quickly dragged the dog in the house and shut the front door.

He turned to me 'your like a bloody curse to me you son!' Harry yelled 'sorry Harry I've brought you these to say I'm sorry!' and I handed him the coop carrier bag full of cans.

He smiled and said 'cheers son'.

'Look if there's anything I can do just name it!' I said as Harry started thinking something over.

'There is something! you can take that dog for a walk he's driving me up the bloody wall'.

I explained I was just about to go take Mick to Bolden but I would soon as I come back.

'Take him with you he loves a ride in the car he'll just sit there with his head out the window and it'll give me a chance to paint the doors without him jumping all over the bloody place'.

'Aye ok no bother' I replied.

My dad came to the front door and said 'what's Fleetwood mac doing here?'.

'He's going to take me for a driving lesson is it ok to borrow the car?' I asked as Harry came out and handed me Rambo on the lead.

'Aye Krusty is taking his car anyway, but be careful!' He said as Rambo began humping my leg.

'Off!' Harry shouted to Him and handed him a dog chew when he did as he was told.

'Don't let him off the lead! and here's some chews he goes mad for them!' He said handing me a bag of spiral sticks.

'Please be careful' he said kissing the dog on the head.

I opened the car rear door and Rambo jumped in and sat on the back seat with his chew in his mouth happily munching away.

'Do you want me to drive?' asked Mick.

'Aye please il drive back' I said jumping in the back with the dog.

We eventually pulled up to a pub in Boldon Colliery next to the train tracks called the Beggars bridge.

I jumped out with Rambo on the lead and we walked into the pub.

Soon as we stepped inside the barmaid shouted 'sorry no dogs!'.

I left with the dog and took him to a patch of grass by a red and white fence where he started sniffing around.

Mick popped his head out the pub door and said 'you want a pint?'

'I better not mate' I replied thinking I can't really leave the dog outside.

After a few minutes I realized I really did need a piss.

I stood there for a few more minutes while Rambo had a dump. I started dragging the dog towards the pub as I really needed the toilet but he was still sniffing away. I decided I was going to tie his lead to the fence while I quickly ran for the bog.

I tied his lead in a double knot and dropped a couple of dog chews down on the grass and ran as quick as I could to the pub.

I seen Mick sat at the bar with some bloke sat next to him with a cap on they were chatting away so I just ran past them and into the toilet.

A few minutes later I ran back out as Mick was shaking hands with the bloke and he quickly downed his pint and followed me outside with his new crank for his bike.

We walked out the door and I looked over to where I'd left the dog and it was gone! Not only the dog but the fence too.

'What the hell?' I shouted and ran to the spot Rambo was last seen.

'Rambo!' I yelled.

'Please don't tell me you tied it to the level crossing barrier!' Said Mick pointing to the raised barrier I'd left the dog tied too.

I couldn't breath I couldn't look up I just started panicking and fell to the ground shaking I looked over and seen two dog chews on the grass and his turd and I almost started crying 'oh my god what have I done!' I screamed.

Mick tried to calm me down putting his hand on my shoulder.

'His leads still on the barrier! Maybe he escaped!' Shouted Mick.

I couldn't think about it I was devastated and burst into tears.

A man in a high vis jacket came over and seen the state I was in and helped me to my feet.
'Did you tie that dog to the Barrier?' He said staring into my tear filled eyes. 'yes' I struggled to say.
'Can you come this way please?' Asked the bloke.
Mick and I followed him. He took us into a little wooden gate house next to the tracks he opened the door and Rambo came running out to greet me.
I fell to my knees grabbed his collar and hugged him and he immediately wiggled loose and began humping my arm.
I reached in my pocket gave him the full bag of chews and he immediately let go and started munching away.
'What the hell possessed you to tie him to the barrier!' Shouted the bloke.
'I had no idea! and I needed a piss' I stuttered smiling just relieved to see Rambo was ok.
'Well it's lucky for you I spotted him there before the gate lifted you bloody idiot'
The bloke shouted.
'I'm sorry' I replied climbing back to my feet and shaking his hand.
'Thank you!' I said.
'Come on let's get his lead' the bloke said and led us outside as I gripped Rambo's collar as tight as I could.

I decided to let Mick drive back as I was in no fit state. I just sat with Rambo in the backseat thinking thank god he's ok.

Epilogue.

My 3 year had flown by! the dockyard group was bought out in 1997 by a company called Cammell Laird most of the lads from Wear Dock were transferred to Hepburn Tyneside.

After finishing our Apprenticeships we were all told we had a job for life at the company and we stayed on as tradesmen for just over a year but unfortunately the company went into administration and hundreds of good men lost their jobs and everyone went their separate ways.

It was the end of an era in many ways for us and the North East as many good men never worked in the industry again.

I remember telling Colin one day that having a trade would open a lot of doors we could work wherever we wanted! it turned out to be true Colin emigrated to Australia and still lives there today with his brother.

He still keeps in touch with his friends and his Mam and of course his real Dad.

Ricky left the game to Pursue a career in music after he finally got over his case of pringles and the smell of rotten fish.

Iain and I still remain close friends and have worked together on various jobs since the dockyard as well as Decka who still remains a great mate who always seems to have my back.

I myself went on to work in many places including Saudi Arabia, France, Norway, Holland as well as many shipyards up and down the UK normally causing chaos wherever I went but that's a story for another day.

The end.

A little note from Frank.

A few of the names have been changed but the characters in this book are based on real characters.
One character in particular 'Blue' wasn't an actual pervert just a genuinely lovely guy but his character is based on lots of lads who work in the dockyard who are like blue the character. I used his nickname only.
Dickie was a real character and exactly as he is in the book lovely guy who I've never seen for years.
Dan (real person top bloke)
Paula (real person poor woman was demented with our escapades as apprentices).

Most of the stories in this book actually happened
the roof, the drug dealers, the crane game
amongst many others and our daily nightmares with JJ who's name I changed slightly. The incident with him and Decka didn't happen and in the end John seemed to change his attitude towards us and became a nice guy and he'd laugh about how thick me and Iain were back in the day.

I'd also like to point out the story line with Dot and Colin was fiction I don't want his wife banging on my door saying 'who's this Pamela and Colin?' Sorry Dot (his name was also changed)

Also my apologies to my neighbor Harry who's garden I wrecked that drunken night (and the cricket bar incident actually happened but it was another neighbor not Harry)

Mrs Patterson my lovely elderly neighbor who sadly passed away not long after this book was set.
RIP x

Decka is based on a real character but didn't actually work in Wear Dockyard or Hepburn although there were many like him.

All of these stories wouldn't have been possible without my Dad 'Basil Fawlty' who was a dead ringer for John Cleese back in the day and is still today one of the funniest guys I've ever known.
He told me a lot of the stories I used in this book and the sequel (if it ever sells I'll give him a cut and pay him back that money for Mrs Patterson's bathroom). Love ya Dad.

I'd also like to thank my Mam for always putting up with my calamities over the years and the puddles left round the house after my drunken nights out with the lads.
Love you mam and thanks for always being there and being the greatest mother I could ever ask for.

I'd also like to thank a million other people but I'd bore you to death but here's a few if you can be arsed to read on:
Trina (love u always and thank you for your continued support and love and kindness).

Pikey: top man my best mate who hardly gets a mention in this book but was another crazy character from the dockyard and a top bloke who's
always there for me in times of trouble.

Jackie you know who you are my brother from another mother a gentleman who would do anything for me my other best friend
(and I'll reveal is who I based the character of Decka)

Iain (character Ian Hunt was based on) My partner in crime at the dockyard who is the funniest man I've ever met and would give you the shirt off his back we need to catch up mate have a sensible few beers. (The poo incident didn't actually happen to Iain it was someone else but it happened)

Natalie and Dave my brother and sister who I love dearly who again are always there for me thank you.

Steve Suttie a cracking author who offered me some invaluable advice thank you your a gentleman and a scholar.

Iain Ayris. The author of my favourite book 'Abide with me' a brilliant author and a lovely bloke who was very happy to offer me advice when I asked Thank you.

Amanda Revell Walton. Another amazing author who was kind enough to offer me some advice when I asked her thank you.

Dylan and Hollie my niece and fella love you and thank you for your kind words of support.

Sam (my nephew and first reviewer of my book ) you gave me confidence to finish the book after your praise of
the early chapters.

(The in laws)  the Murray family thank you all for your continued support over the years and if this book ever gets made into the TV drama (which I originally had planned for it) I'd love Dave Murray to write the theme tune he's such an unbelievable fantastic songwriter and musician. YouTube 'the mackemfolksinger'

Adam (young Frank) my son who I love so much you make me so proud every day.

(The lads at the dockyard) although a lot of the names were changed this book wouldn't have ever been written without you all
I've never laughed so much as at my time at Wear dock 97 and Hepburn (98-2001)
Some great blokes and some downright hilarious characters.

A few of the lads walking down the bank to tune tees Dockyard Hepburn.

The Apprentices at Tyne Tees Dockyard 1998.

whoopa napper (I'm sorry) just kidding there isn't a whopper napper he was a fictional character I made up with all those people in mind I've met over the years no matter how hard I try I just can't get on with (mind you there is a pipefitter out there somewhere with the nickname but I've never actually met him) but I've heard he's a nice guy not like the Twat in the book.

Robbie thank you mate (I won't let you forget the kindness you shown when I was penniless and you bought me a ticket for that Bob Marley tribute in Falmouth) and Billy smart who offered to pay for my digs while working away skint.
I meet people like Robbie all the time genuinely nice people who are always happy to help out less fortunate people. Also Nathan Black another cracking lad who'd give you the shirt off his back as well as being a comedy genius who makes my throat hurt after a shift here in France with all his jokes and antics.
I really hope I haven't forgotten anyone but if I have this is for you too.

Tracey who was like the mother of the contractors working in Portsmouth (not old enough to be our mother) but made us all feel like we had a home away from home thank you.

Someone else I'd like to thank is the other Tracey who we all pestered to fax our expenses off who never complained and always had a smile on her face and cakes to give away thank you.

Alan Armstrong RIP a former work colleague and friend sadly missed top bloke.

Robert Lowery another top bloke a fellow contractor and friend who sadly passed away top bloke.

Tommy Stores my old boss at Hepburn lovely bloke who was a big loss to everyone back then and a big miss.

Frode a lad I met on a flight in Norway who happily shared his vodka with me when I was sitting there terrified (RIP mate)

To all my friends I've met over the years I'm sorry if your names don't get a mention I've met so many amazing people I could go on forever thank you all.

My Dad Dot Pikey and a few others.